'Where's the menu, then, Mike?'

As Mike hurried away to collect it from the bar Ross said, 'Mike Gurdon's the owner and, I warn you, he doesn't need any encouragement.'

Beth's eyes widened with disbelief. 'Encouragement? I only asked him to use the name everyone else knows me by.' She knew he hadn't missed the fact that her cheeks were flaring with colour and wondered if he believed that it gave the lie to her denial.

'Fine. I just wanted you to know what to expect.'

What did Ross think she was—a raving nymphomaniac?

Born in the industrial north, **Sheila Danton** trained as a Registered General Nurse in London before joining the Air Force nursing service. Her career was interrupted by marriage, three children, and a move to the West Country, where she now lives. She soon returned to her chosen career, training and specialising in Occupational Health, with an interest in preventive medicine. Sheila has now taken early retirement and is thrilled to be able to write full-time.

Recent titles by the same author:

MONSOONS APART
BASE PRINCIPLES

PRESCRIPTION FOR CHANGE

BY
SHEILA DANTON

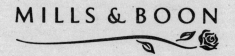

*MILLS & BOON, the Rose Device and
LOVE ON CALL are trademarks of the publisher.
Harlequin Mills & Boon Limited,
Eton House, 18-24 Paradise Road, Richmond, Surrey TW9 1SR
This edition published by arrangement with Harlequin Enterprises B.V.*

© Sheila Danton 1995

ISBN 0 263 79457 1

*Set in Times 11 on 12½ pt. by
Rowland Phototypesetting Limited
Bury St Edmunds, Suffolk*

03-9601-38493

*Made and printed in Great Britain
Cover illustration by Simon Bishop*

CHAPTER ONE

'IF WE offer you the position would it be possible for you to start immediately?'

Sensing that the practice manager was indicating that the job was hers if she wanted it, Beth felt a tingle of optimism surge through her body. This was the chance she needed to put the past behind her once and for all.

'Well, almost,' she replied. 'I—er—I have a commitment to the agency for tomorrow, but would Friday morning be all right?'

'More than we dared hope for.' Dr David Murrin, the younger of the two junior partners, smiled at her. 'We've been coping far too long without a nurse.'

The other two interviewers nodded their agreement.

'At least, we all think so,' the female doctor contributed. 'Dr McKava is happy to continue as we are. He says if he does everything himself he knows it's done properly.'

So that was why the senior partner was not at the interview. The manager had said that he'd been called out on an emergency, but Beth now guessed that that was a cover-up. She'd met Dr McKava's type before. No doubt he was one of the old school, nearing retirement and unwilling to change.

'If appointed, I'll do my best to convert him for you,' she told them confidently, her deep blue eyes shining.

The practice manager offered her a welcoming hand. 'I think we've already decided that you're the person to do that if anyone can. But be warned. It won't be easy.' Pushing her chair back, she asked, 'Can you spare a few minutes for me to show you the geography of the place? I'm Laura, by the way.'

Beth nodded. 'No problem. I'm not working at all today.'

'This will be your base.' Laura led the way from the tiny conference-room into a spacious treatment-room with a smell of new wood and paint that was almost intoxicating. Beth moved carefully from cupboard to cupboard, her eyes wide with amazement. Every piece of equipment she had begged for in her previous practice was there, much of it apparently unused. What a waste.

'How long have you been without a nurse?' she asked, wondering how difficult it was going to be to re-establish the position.

'Our last one left the week we moved into this building. That was nearly ten weeks ago. We do have one who comes in on a sessional basis, usually in the evenings, but she doesn't want to work full-time.'

'The nurse who left must have been disappointed to miss the chance of working here. I know I would have been.'

'Possibly.' Laura shrugged and moved on quickly, saying, 'This is the record store — accessed from Reception and by this security door.' She punched a combination of numbers into the lock and pushed the door open.

'The male racks start against the wall, alphabetically, and the female by the window.'

Beth tried to take it all in, but she knew she was bound to forget something.

'This is Reception — Joanne works here afternoons and evenings.'

Beth gave the young girl a friendly nod and followed Laura through to her office.

'I'm sorry to rush you, but I do have another meeting to attend.' She handed Beth a bunch of keys. 'The big ones are the front door and treatment-room keys. The remainder are for your various cupboards. We only unlocked them for the interviews.' She handed Beth the keys and also a printed card. 'That's the present record store code. It changes occasionally, but never without warning.'

Beth felt as if she was walking on air as she left the Windber family practice. A brand-new building, pleasant colleagues — everything she'd hoped for, and more.

She was so engrossed in her own thoughts that she didn't see the dark-haired man in an ultra-smart suit lifting his briefcase from the boot of a dark blue BMW. As he swung it round on to the ground Beth fell over it. Feeling a complete fool, she picked herself up, muttered an apology and rushed away.

She heard him call something after her but ignored it. Reps were synonymous with trouble in her life, and with everything starting to go right for her at last the best way to deal with him was to pretend that he didn't exist.

She climbed quickly into her red Fiesta and, without a backward glance, drove out of the car park.

On Friday morning Beth donned her blue uniform and fastened the belt round her waist with the buckle that Richard had bought her on the day she'd passed her finals. Then, sweeping her shoulder-length hair back with a neat clasp, she set out to start her new career.

She knew she was early, but wanted to organise the treatment-room to her way of working before patients started to arrive.

As the main door was locked, she presumed that she was the first to arrive and let herself in with the doorkey given to her by the practice manager. She was happily rearranging the first cupboard when she thought she heard a noise across in the record store.

Intending to announce her presence, she moved into the reception area and peered through the glass screen. She saw a dark-haired giant of a man purposefully running a finger along the shelves of notes.

She swallowed hard. He was dressed in crumpled jeans and an old sweater, and, being unshaven, with tousled hair, he presented a frightening appearance, especially as he had the physique of a wrestler. Sure that he must be an intruder, Beth knew it was her duty to prevent him locating whatever confidential information he was searching for so diligently.

Drawing herself up to her full height, even though she knew he would tower above her, she took the code card the practice manager had given her and punched in the number specified. The man turned at the click and Beth's gaze met a pair of dark, brooding eyes. The eyebrows above them rose despairingly as he recognised that he'd been caught out by a nurse.

'Hello. I'm Beth Linkirk.' Her voice was quiet. She knew the last thing she should do was rush in and antagonise him. 'Can I help you? Are you looking for something?' All the time she was talking she moved slowly forward, increasingly aware of his overwhelming masculinity. As she finished speaking she took a firm hold of the arm that had just found what he was looking for.

'What the hell are you playing at?' His bellow echoed through the empty waiting-room as his muscular arm attempted to shake off her limpet-like grip.

Despite its ear-splitting level she was surprised by the cultivated timbre of his voice. She murmured soothingly, 'Let's just sit down and talk about it, shall we? Over——'

'Dr McKava! Sister Linkirk! What on earth is happening?' Laura was staring at the scene before her as if unable to believe her eyes.

Beth felt her jaw dropping. Dr McKava! The senior partner? It couldn't be! He was older, about to retire surely! Wasn't he? For the first time she considered the awful notion that her image of him might have been wrong. 'I—er—I thought you had broken in,' she gabbled breathlessly.

He shrugged himself from her grasp. 'I don't believe it! Saints preserve me from interfering nurses who jump to the wrong conclusions.' He snatched the notes he wanted from the shelf and strode from the room, muttering, 'The community's the place for nurses, not under my feet.'

'What have you done?' Laura was distraught. 'I thought you were going to try and persuade Ross to work with a practice nurse.'

'He looked more like a down-and-out,' Beth defended herself hotly. 'How was I to know who he was?' She gave a nervous giggle. 'I actually thought he was one of your homeless psychiatric patients.'

Despite her obvious apprehension at the doctor's reaction Laura couldn't help but laugh. 'I don't think you'd better tell *him* that. Poor chap's been on call and obviously hasn't seen much of his bed.'

Beth decided that the sooner she retreated to the safety of her own room the better.

But a refuge it was not. The commanding figure of Ross McKava was rooting carelessly through the one cupboard she had so far rearranged.

She took a deep breath and counted to five. 'Can I help you?' she asked quietly.

He turned to glare at her as if she were persecuting him. 'I'm perfectly capable of finding what I want, thank you, *Sister*.' He stressed her title aggressively. 'I've done it often enough.'

Beth lowered her fair eyelashes meekly. 'But I've moved things around. I——'

'Have come here to disrupt everything,' he finished for her. 'Show me where the nebuliser is, then. I've an asthmatic patient waiting.'

Beth was tempted to say that as asthmatics needed an atmosphere of calm the patient might be better off without him. However, she thought better of it and handed him the portable atomiser together with the capsules containing the drugs he might need.

His hand brushed hers as he took them from her and she was conscious of his interest as his fingers encountered her wedding-ring.

He lifted his head and studied her as if seeing her for the first time. 'Have you any patients waiting, Sister?'

She shook her head. 'Not that I know of.'

'Right. As you've nothing better to do you can come with me. You might just be able to help. This child has never used a nebuliser before.'

Startled, Beth was about to argue when she thought better of it. Especially after her earlier gaffe. She followed him out of the treatment-room and, passing Laura in the corridor, just had time to murmur, 'Dr McKava wants me to help him with a home visit. Don't know when I'll be back,' before he snapped impatiently,

'*Do* come on; we're wasting valuable time.'

Once outside, she took the equipment from him again and climbed into the passenger seat of his dark blue BMW. Before she had her seatbelt fastened they were leaving the car park and heading out of town. 'Where are we going?'

He pushed the notes he had collected across to her. 'Windber Gate Estate—a huge new development that's already overburdening our practice.'

'Couldn't you take on another partner?' Beth asked tentatively as she quickly scanned the personal details of the patient.

'If only it were so easy! Most of the patients will transfer when the new health centre opens on the estate next year. Then we'd be left with too many doctors.'

As he spoke he glanced repeatedly across at her, seemingly puzzled. He suddenly let out a small gasp of triumph. 'I know where I've seen you before. I do believe we met in the car park on Wednesday. Well, not exactly met. You aimed a well-directed kick at my case and left without introducing yourself.'

Recalling the incident only too well, Beth responded defensively, 'I didn't kick it. You swung round unexpectedly and plonked it in my path. There was no way I could avoid it.'

She had been so determined that no one would spoil her new-found contentment that day that she hadn't really looked at him. Now, as she searched his profile, she saw a hint of a grin wipe the weariness from his features and was impressed by what she saw. His dark hair was well cut above his ears and when he had a chance to smarten himself up she guessed that he'd be quite something to look at. Not that she was interested. After her late husband's behaviour men did not figure in her plans for the future.

Sensing her silent scrutiny, he asked, 'So why did you ignore me when I tried to make amends?'

Conscious of the heat flooding her cheeks, Beth murmured, 'I—I felt a fool. I—I should have been watching where I was going.'

'Mmm. And?' He didn't sound convinced.

In desperation Beth added, 'I—er—thought you were a rep.'

The moment she'd uttered the words she knew they'd been a mistake.

'So? Don't you speak to reps?'

Beth hesitated before replying. 'Yes, but, well, I know it sounds odd, but. . .' Her voice tailed off. How could she explain her behaviour without revealing the events that must remain hidden if she was to make a success of this fresh start?

Luckily she didn't have to. The car was already at a standstill in front of a house so newly built that the garden was a rocky wilderness. His question forgotten, he ordered, 'Come on. Show me what you're capable of.'

The child's mother must have been watching for them. She opened the door immediately, an anxious look on her face.

'She's not any better, Doctor,' she called tearfully. 'I don't know what to do.'

As he strode into the downstairs front room Beth took the mother's arm. 'But we do, so why don't you go and make us all a nice cup of tea? I shouldn't think the doctor had time for any breakfast.'

As Mrs Rennell went hesitantly to do what Beth had suggested Beth returned to the front room.

Kylie, the patient, was so small and emaciated that Beth found it difficult to believe that she was the eleven-year-old that the notes referred to. Beth crouched before her and gently smoothed the girl's dishevelled hair back from her forehead.

She was leaning forward on her arms, an oxygen mask half on and half off her face, but still not able to get the breath out of her lungs. The doctor was already priming the nebuliser.

'Have you given anything systemically?'

He nodded. 'I gave her a couple of injections when I was here earlier.' He lowered his voice.

'I think we're winning. Despite what her mother says the wheeze is nowhere near so pronounced, so I think now's the time for her to learn how to use the nebuliser.'

Mrs Rennell came into the room with a tray of tea. Kylie's wheeze immediately became louder and she rested her head trustingly against Beth's chest.

Dr McKava indicated that they should stay where they were and, helping himself to a cup of tea, motioned the girl's mother to join him in the hall. Kylie's breathing immediately became easier.

Beth chatted soothingly to the girl. 'That's better. Is this your teddy?' She retrieved an obviously much loved bear from the floor. Kylie nodded, and moved a hand to clasp the bear to her cheek. 'He looks an old friend. Have you had him since you were a baby?'

Again the girl nodded, but her eyes swivelled anxiously to watch her mother returning to her side. Beth flashed them both a reassuring smile. 'Much better now, aren't you, Kylie?' For the first time the girl smiled and Beth saw her mother visibly relax.

'I'll leave Sister with you for the moment, and come back for her later.' Beth hadn't expected that from the doctor and was about to protest when he continued, 'If you come to the car, Sister, I'll give you the bits and pieces you might need.'

As they reached the driver's door of the BMW she asked with a frown, 'Shouldn't I be seeing patients in the surgery?'

'They can manage without you for one more day. You're more use here at the moment.'

Wondering if this was his way of keeping her out of the treatment-room, she asked, 'So what else do I need?'

'Nothing,' he replied shortly, 'but I saw you were about to argue and wanted to put you in the picture. Mother's over-anxious and over-protective because Father walked out almost the moment they moved into this house.'

'I noticed Kylie's wheezing gets worse every time her mother puts in an appearance. So what do you want me to do?'

'Just keep the situation calm until I can alert our social worker, Mary Banks.'

'Social worker?'

'Yes. Kylie's mother isn't coping without Dad, and she desperately needs to get a few practicalities sorted out. She has no money coming in at the moment and the rent is mounting up.'

Beth nodded. 'I understand.'

'When you think it's feasible check Kylie's peak flow-rate. She has her own meter. Get her to use the nebuliser again and show the mother how it works. I explained to Mrs Rennell that it does the same job as the inhaler spray but more efficiently. And when you think the time's right show them how to use a spacer device to increase the amount of the drug reaching her lungs from her aerosols.'

Beth nodded. 'It'll be half the battle won if we can give them both confidence that they can handle any further attacks.'

He scribbled a prescription. 'Send Mother out for a walk to get this spacer and I think you'll find the break will do them both good. I'll be back about eleven.'

Beth returned to the front room of the house, pleased that, after watching her in action, he appeared to trust her to do the right thing. In this case, anyway.

'Dr McKava didn't have what he needed in the car. Could you get round to the chemist and collect this while I look after Kylie?'

Beth had no idea where the nearest chemist was situated and she could see that Mrs Rennell was torn. She didn't want to leave her sick child, but neither did she want to be left alone with her in case the attack got worse. Her fear won the day and, kissing Kylie, she reassured her, 'I won't be long, love.'

When Kylie had settled down again, Beth suggested, 'Before we do anything more, we ought to check how much air you can blow out. Dr McKava says you have a flowmeter.'

Kylie nodded, unearthed the instrument from beneath a pile of clothes on the chair beside her and, zeroing the pointer, blew as hard as she could.

Beth took the meter from her and nodded encouragingly. 'Not bad, considering. We'll try again later.'

She freshened up the little girl's hands and face with a flannel soaked in hot water, and then brushed her hair for her. 'What lovely hair, Kylie. Are you growing it?'

The little girl nodded shyly. 'Yours is nice too. How long is it?' She asked the question with only a hint of a wheeze.

'When it's loose it falls just below my shoulders.' She turned so that Kylie could see the length of her honey-coloured ponytail.

'That's how I'd like mine.' She was more animated now, so Beth took the opportunity to give her a drink.

'Lemonade all right?'

Kylie nodded. 'I prefer cold drinks.' She wrinkled her nose. 'I don't like coffee or tea.'

Beth squatted down beside her while she drank. 'Neither do I most of the time. I drink them to be sociable.'

By the time Mrs Rennell returned they were firm friends, and Kylie's wheeze was barely audible. It was a good opportunity to test her peak flow-rate again, and then to demonstrate to them both how the spacer should be used.

Despite the impression that Ross McKava had made on her earlier, when he returned at eleven Beth couldn't believe the transformation. He'd washed and shaved and the dark suit he was wearing gave him such a presence that her heart flipped uncomfortably. She'd thought him attractive enough in his casual clothes, but now he was downright handsome, and radiated a warm masculinity that stirred her senses despite herself.

Even Kylie's mother seemed more relaxed with him in his usual working clothes, and when he introduced Mary Banks, the social worker who arrived soon afterwards, Mrs Rennell's gratitude for all he'd done was overwhelming.

However, when they made to leave she followed them to the door, her anxiety resurfacing. 'Will Kylie need anything else?'

'Sister will pop back at two and see that you are doing things correctly,' the doctor assured her, and was rewarded by seeing Mrs Rennell's relief, so he added, 'Ring the surgery if you need me before that.'

As she took her seat beside him in the luxurious car Beth asked, 'What if I have patients booked in to see me at two?'

'You won't have. I popped in earlier and told Laura you might not be available all day as you were doing what nurses should do—nurse.'

Astounded, Beth stammered, 'An—and what did Laura say to that?'

He grinned. 'She said you weren't employed as a community nurse, but when I told her how well you were doing she agreed you should continue.'

She guessed his compliment was intended to undermine any protest, leaving her even more suspicious of his motives. It seemed that he was deliberately keeping her out of the surgery.

As she tried to work out the best method of attack her silence prompted him to ask, 'Is there a problem, Bethany?'

Although wondering how his partners felt about her absence from the treatment-room, she guessed that now was not the time to voice her query and asked instead, 'How do you know I'm called Bethany?'

He seemed surprised by the question. 'I saw your application form, of course.'

She would have left it there had he not then said, 'But I do wonder why you don't acknowledge your married status.'

She knew he was referring to the title Ms, which she had used when applying. 'Men don't, so why should I?'

'What do you mean?'

'If I advertise a job and you and two other men apply I have no way of knowing which of you are married and which aren't, because you would all use the title Mr.'

'I wouldn't,' he joked. 'I'd use Dr.'

Annoyed that he wasn't taking her seriously, she retorted, 'I was speaking hypothetically and you know it.'

He shrugged. 'So you're a women's libber as well, then?'

'Why do I have to be labelled? I'm an individual and want to be treated like one.'

She was relieved when he didn't pursue the subject of her marital status. Her private life was just that—private. She would never forget the past, but with nothing or no one to remind her she could learn to live with it.

'What are you going to do with the rest of your morning?'

His deep voice broke in on her reverie, so, to give herself a chance to regain control, she checked her watch.

'There's not much morning left! I suppose if there are no patients for me to see I'll reorganise the remainder of the cupboards until it's time to visit Kylie again.'

Expecting her proposal to annoy him, she was surprised when he asked, 'What did you think of Kylie?'

'She's lovely, but she needs stability in her life.'

'I couldn't agree more, but the mother's confidence has been eroded by her husband's departure, especially as she can't see how she is going to manage financially.'

'No doubt that's part of Kylie's problem.'

He nodded. 'She misses him desperately. It could take years for her to accept it, if she ever does.'

'And, in the meantime, Kylie will go on having these attacks?'

'I don't know. When I came back to collect you I sensed a new determination in them both.

Learning to use the spacer probably has something to do with it.'

'I guess that knowing they can cope, even with the bad attacks, is as important as the drugs you prescribe.'

'It certainly is. And with the number of new cases rising all the time it's going to be even more important.' He turned into his parking space at the rear of the practice buildings.

Sensing that here was a way she could perhaps prove her worth, Beth said, 'I used to run an asthma-management clinic at my last practice and it was a great success—for all of us.' Her resolve not to antagonise him was forgotten in her passion for the project which had been her idea. 'The patients and their families were happy because they could see me at any time and I drew up management plans with them, making them confident that they could cope. The doctors were happy because they weren't called out so often. You see——'

'I see that if we let you get your way you'll change Windber practice beyond recognition,' he interrupted curtly. 'Well, I'm sorry, but I like to check my asthmatic patients personally—and I can assure you I do it regularly.'

CHAPTER TWO

RECOGNISING that she had allowed her enthusiasm to run away with her, Beth tried to make amends. 'I didn't intend——' He'd pulled the car into his parking space and climbed out before she could finish the sentence.

As he strode silently into the practice reception area she followed him, her mood thoughtful. She wasn't going to convert him to the idea of a practice nurse if she went on as she had started—first mistaking him for an intruder and then committing the cardinal sin of insinuating how much better the last practice she'd worked for had done things.

Her intention had been to show him that she could lighten his workload, but he'd believed that she was criticising his handling of his patients. If only she hadn't been so insensitive her success with Kylie might have gone some way to converting him to the idea of working with a practice nurse.

As it was she had made matters worse. The touchiness in his manner, which throughout the morning had prevented her from being totally at ease with him, was now replaced by outright hostility.

'Can you help with the antenatal clinic this afternoon?'

Beth had been so absorbed in her thoughts that she hadn't heard Laura come into the room behind her.

'What time's that?'

'Three till about five—with Liz.'

'Dr McKava wants me to visit the patient we saw this morning about two, but all being well I should be back.'

'Good.' Laura raised a surprised eyebrow but didn't comment further. She was obviously used to the senior partner's unconventional demands.

'Oh, by the way, I was going to ask. . .' Laura nibbled at her bottom lip.

Wondering what was coming, Beth asked, 'Was there something else?'

'Would you mind staying on for evening surgery today? The part-time nurse has just phoned in sick.'

'No problem.'

She smiled at Laura, who replied darkly, 'I hope not, but you will be working with Ross.'

'Dr McKava? And?' Beth prompted.

'He won't like it if you see patients he hasn't referred to you himself.'

'You mean if someone comes in and asks to see me I have to refuse—however long they may have to wait for him?'

'That's about it.'

'Waste of time me being here, then.' Beth was irritated.

'Not really. He'll send patients through to you for injections, dressings, phlebotomy, even ear-syringeing, but he wants to see them first.'

Beth shook her head despairingly. 'Why did no one say this at the interview?'

'Because the others are quite happy for you to see as many patients as you have time for, and some besides! And once Ross accepts that you're a skilled practitioner I'm sure he will be as well. As long as you don't rush in and do the wrong thing first!' Laura smiled unconvincingly, leaving Beth feeling even more uneasy.

Surely he couldn't think her that useless if he was happy for her to go back and see Kylie alone? Although, thinking about it, she supposed that she was only carrying out his instructions. He'd made it more than clear that that was all she was to do.

Well, if that was the way he wanted it, so be it. It was going to be a long first day and by five o'clock she would probably welcome an easy session.

Not knowing how long a break she would get for lunch, Beth had brought a sandwich, which she consumed in her room before setting out on her visit.

Kylie's condition was unchanged, and her delighted mother, after a long chat with the social worker and contact with a solicitor specialising in marriage breakdown, had begun to see that there could possibly be a better future than she had imagined.

'Thank you for all your help, Sister. And for the doctor's. You've both been so kind.'

'Don't hesitate to ring in again if you're worried.'

Kylie gave her a shy smile and handed her a piece of paper. 'It's a poem. I've just written it. I'd like you to have it.'

Beth unfolded the paper and read:

> The doctor came to me today,
> He brought a lady too.
> She had long wavy hair that shone
> Like gold, and eyes of blue.

'Why, that's lovely, Kylie. Is this your hobby?' The girl nodded, pleased by Beth's approval. 'I like reading and writing poetry myself when I have time. I'll treasure this always.' She bent and kissed the little girl's cheek. 'Thank you. I'll look forward to reading more of your poems.'

She made her way back to the surgery with a warm feeling. She couldn't take the credit for encouraging Kylie to write, but she'd obviously made an impression on the youngster and if the girl could keep up her interest in writing it would take her mind off the problems at home, and might even help her to come to terms with some of them.

Liz Harsham was just starting the antenatals when she arrived. 'Good to see you, Beth. Would you do the weighing and blood-pressures? And they should all have brought a specimen of urine for testing. If you write the results on the co-operation card that they should all have with them I'll transfer them to the notes when I've examined them.'

Beth knew all about antenatal clinics. She'd enjoyed doing them in her last job, especially during those last few months when she herself had been pregnant.

Pushing the poignant thought of her stillborn daughter to the back of her mind, she sighed as she called out the name of the first mother-to-be on her list and greeted her patient warmly.

The clinic ran late, and the evening patients had started to arrive before the senior partner put in an appearance.

'All well?' he asked as Liz came to collect the last antenatal from Beth.

They both nodded. 'We're just finishing,' Liz said, then disappeared along the corridor.

He looked around the treatment-room. 'Where's Helen?'

'If she's the usual evening nurse, she's off sick,' Beth informed him. 'I've offered to stay on.'

'There's no need. I can manage and you've had a long day already.'

Resentment at his continued efforts to prevent her doing the work she was employed to do made

Beth argue. 'So have you. *And* you were up all last night.'

'I've had a sleep this afternoon,' he informed her shortly. 'Haven't you a family to get home to?'

'No! So I'll stay for now and if it gets too much for me I'll go home. OK?'

If looks were anything to go by it was anything but. However, he didn't say so, just shut himself into his consulting-room.

Did he think her so incapable that he was better off without her help? Or, having noted her wedding-ring, did he think she was neglecting her family? Whichever, having got her foot into the doorway of the treatment-room she was staying there.

She dealt quickly but confidently with the first few patients he sent through to her. Two were for tetanus injections, one for a dressing, and one needed his ears syringed. In between she familiarised herself with other parts of the building and the evening staff.

It was while she was talking to the receptionist, Joanne, that a mother came in clutching a young baby. It was obvious that she was near to tears.

'I must see the doctor tonight. I'm Mrs Cavington. Iris.'

'Is it for you or the baby?' Joanne asked quietly.

'Me—for both of us really.' The mother gave a tearful hiccup. 'For me and Jason.'

'Dr McKava is fully booked for this evening,' Joanne replied, quietly soothing. 'Er—if it's an emergency he'll see you at the end of surgery. That'll mean a long wait, though, so if it's not an emergency why don't you come back in the morning?'

The tears that had been threatening came in full flood then. 'I can't wait that long. I've left my two-year-old with a neighbour.'

Beth motioned to Joanne that she would see her in the treatment-room and ignored the warning in Joanne's eyes. 'Can you let me have the notes for both of them?' she whispered before ushering the woman through.

Closing the door, she asked quietly, 'Would you like me to hold the baby?'

Mrs Cavington clutched him even closer to her body. 'I'm gonna die and leave him soon enough.'

'What on earth makes you think that?'

She sniffed miserably. 'I was feeding him tonight. It's not been comfortable for a couple of days and then I saw it.'

'Saw what?'

'The lump. In my left breast. I don't want to die and leave him.' The tears were joined by an unhappy wail.

Beth placed an arm round the patient's shoulders. 'Mrs Cavington, it's most unlikely that the lump is what you think it is, and even if it is you're not going to die. Not with today's treatments. Now, how about letting me hold the baby for a moment while you go behind the curtain and undress?'

Mrs Cavington thought for a moment, then decided that knowing would surely be better than not knowing, and handed over her son.

As she undressed Beth cuddled Jason close. 'He's gorgeous.' Refusing to allow her own feelings of loss to overwhelm her, she asked, 'How old is he?'

'Six weeks,' came the tearful response from behind the curtain. 'I'm ready, Nurse.'

Beth joined her and, returning the baby to its rightful owner, gently proceeded to examine the very engorged breast where Mrs Cavington indicated. She wasn't at all surprised to see that the area was red and hot and very tender.

'I'm not the doctor, but I'd say it's an abscess. Quite common in mothers who produce a lot of milk.'

'Do you really think that's all it is, Nurse?' Mrs Cavington was only too ready to substitute hope for fear, but Beth had to be practical.

'As I said, I'm not the expert. I'll catch Dr McKava between patients and let him have a look at you. In the meantime keep yourself warm with this dressing-gown.' She handed her a towelling robe from the back of the door.

His consulting-room door opened at that moment, so before he could call in the next appointment she slipped in, taking Mrs Cavington's notes with her.

He looked up impatiently. 'Yes? I hope this is important. I'm behind already.'

'Very important. I have Mrs Cavington and her six-week-old baby in the treatment-room and think she has a breast abscess. You need to see her before you see your next appointment.'

He subjected her to a long, silent stare before saying coldly, 'What is she doing in your room?'

Beth tried to hide her exasperation. 'She hadn't an appointment, so I was trying to save you time by getting her undressed.'

Without a word he rose from his seat and strode across to the treatment-room. Beth followed gingerly and was surprised by the change in his demeanour as he gently took the baby from Mrs Cavington's arms and handed him to Beth. 'Take care of this precious bundle for us.'

He asked the patient a few questions, then examined her gently. 'It is a breast abscess, as I gather Sister thought. We'll need to get you a breast-pump to get rid of the milk. In the meantime, if it's too painful, we'll show you how to express the milk yourself.

'I'll give you an antibiotic that should soon have the infection under control, but we need to keep an eye on you until it is. Slip the dressing-gown on while Sister brings your son to collect the prescription from my room.'

Carrying the now dozing baby, Beth followed him across the corridor and waited silently for him to write the prescription. As he handed her the piece of paper his gaze rested warmly on the child sleeping comfortably in her arms, and when he momentarily lifted his eyes Beth was sure she saw a momentary longing there.

However, it didn't last and, mentally shaking himself back into the task in hand, he pressed the button to call his next patient through before saying, 'Thank you for what you did, but don't let your success go to your head. As I told you earlier, I prefer to see all my patients personally.'

His next patient was already coming into the room, so Beth swallowed the retort she was about to make and returned to the treatment-room.

'Will you be able to get these this evening?' she asked as she handed Mrs Cavington the prescription.

Freed from her earlier anxiety, the patient smiled and nodded. 'The chemist stays open until seven.'

'Right, if you could take Jason, I think I saw a breast-pump in one of my cupboards.'

'Will these tablets not hurt the baby?'

Beth shook her head emphatically. 'No. Flu-cloxacillin is a safe antibiotic for breast-feeding mums and their babies. Ah, here's the pump. Brand-new. We'd better try it out.'

They read the instructions together, but when Beth tried it on the affected breast the pain was too great for her patient to bear.

'Not to worry,' Beth told her. 'I'll show you how to do it by hand until the pain is less. We can use this disposable bowl to catch it as it's probably a good idea not to give Jason the milk from that breast for a couple of days, but you must still express the milk regularly.'

Beth carefully expressed a small quantity of the milk, then taught Mrs Cavington how to do it.

'You've got a gentle touch, Nurse—or was it Sister that the doctor called you?'

Beth grinned. 'I answer to either.'

'I suppose you're so good because you've been through all this palaver yourself.'

Beth joked to prevent Mrs Cavington recognising just how much she wished she had. 'I'm afraid not. Put it down to learning to milk the cows at home as a young girl.'

'You're a farmer's daughter?'

Concentrating on her task, Beth nodded.

'Oh, don't you miss it? I always wanted to live on a farm.'

'Farm life is harder than most people think.'

'Oh, I didn't mean——'

Jason woke at that moment and, after apparently watching all his lovely food being wasted, yelled his disgust.

'There's plenty more on the other side, old chap.' Her fears allayed, Mrs Cavington was beaming with delight. 'Is it all right for me to feed him here, Sister?'

'Please do.' Beth nodded and left them alone behind the curtain. Having written up all her records, she wandered along to see what Joanne was up to.

'Mrs Cavington staying the night?' the receptionist joked.

'She's feeding the baby then she'll be away, but first I need to arrange a time to check her tomorrow.'

'Oh, that's been dealt with. Ross told me to put her down for a home visit. From himself.'

Beth's look must have spoken volumes for Joanne placed a consoling hand on her arm. 'He's always like this—has been since——' She stopped and obviously changed what she had been about to say. 'Well, since I've been here.'

Beth shrugged. 'I'll not rock the boat this evening, Joanne, but I can tell you I'm used to being more than a handmaiden to the doctor, and if I'm to stay there need to be a few changes around here.'

A soft footfall made Beth spin round to find Dr McKava there with a patient. 'Can you help Mrs Wellburn fix her new wrist splints?'

Unsure whether he had overheard what she had said, Beth murmured, 'I think I could just about manage that.'

Ignoring her sarcasm, he turned his attention to Mrs Cavington and Jason, who were just leaving. 'I'll see you both tomorrow.'

'What have you been doing?' Beth asked as she prepared the splints Mrs Wellburn had brought with her.

'Dr McKava said he thinks I've been working in a bad position on my DSE.'

'DSE?' Beth queried.

'Display Screen Equipment—what they used to call VDUs. Computer keyboard, really.'

Beth nodded her understanding.

'The doctor told me to get these and bring them back today so he could show me how to use them.'

'What a pity he didn't know I was starting today. It would have saved your and his time if you'd come directly to me. I should do that next time.'

Mrs Wellburn looked sheepish. 'Well—er— the doctor wants to see me himself next Friday. He said I should make the appointment before I leave.'

Beth didn't want to undermine the patient's confidence, so smiled reassuringly. 'I can understand that. He'll want to see for himself how you're responding to treatment.'

The evening surgery continued for another three quarters of an hour, and although he passed several of his patients on to Beth it was always for some prescribed treatment. Nothing was left to her own judgement.

When she was next free she said to Joanne, 'It's pointless them paying for someone with my qualifications.'

The receptionist seemed ill at ease. 'These days Dr McKava doesn't seem to trust anyone to do things without his say-so.'

'You mean he once did?'

'Oh, yes! When his ex-fiancée worked here it

was different. Mind, she was a good nurse, I'll give her that.'

Hearing the consulting-room door open, Beth waited until the last patient had gone through to ask, 'Why did they break up?'

'He wanted a full-time wife and mother. She was too much of a high-flier to agree to that.'

Beth frowned as Joanne slipped her coat on over her uniform. 'Couldn't they have compromised?'

Joanne shrugged. 'Don't ask me. They didn't and that was that. I'm off home now. Lock the door behind me if you're staying.'

Joanne's information made her determined to stay and let Ross McKava know she was just as capable as her predecessor.

However, he forestalled her, saying, 'I'm sorry to have kept you so late, especially when there was so little for you to do. But I did warn you.'

Angry now, Beth replied, 'It was worth it if only to set Mrs Cavington's mind at rest. She was distraught when she came in and Joanne was prepared to turn her away or make her wait until the end of surgery.'

'Which is exactly what she should have done——'

'Such compassion!'

Beth recognised that this time her sarcasm wasn't lost on him. The warmth disappeared from his eyes, changing them to a piercing black that made her uncomfortable.

'If you'd let me finish. . . Joanne has instructions to do just that. Suppose twenty patients came in one evening demanding immediate attention and she pushed them all in between appointments? It would be chaos—and so unfair to those who'd booked——'

'That's a ridiculous hypothesis——'

'Maybe, but word would soon get around if we started down that track.'

Beth opened her mouth to argue further, but he raised a delaying hand.

'However, I was going to say that I'm glad you were there tonight because Mrs Cavington's problem *was* urgent. It would have been unthinkably cruel to keep someone in her state waiting.'

'How do you know what state she was in when she came in?'

His eyes glittered dangerously. 'Joanne told me, of course. And if you hadn't been there Joanne would have let me know the situation and I'd have found a way to see Mrs Cavington as soon as possible.'

Oh!' Beth's cheeks flamed as she realised her mistake. Mortified, she picked up her bag and jacket and tried to escape.

'Now, did you mean it when you said no one was waiting at home?' His voice was suddenly several shades warmer.

Beth shook her head. 'Not this evening.' She wasn't going to lower her defences enough to admit that there never would be.

'In that case I think we deserve a bite to eat without preparing it ourselves. How about it? It's been a hard day for us both.'

Shaken by the way he had turned her criticism around, and then invited her to join him for a meal, Beth answered cautiously, 'That sounds nice, but don't you want to get home?'

He shrugged. 'I have a house, but not a home.'

'What do you mean by that?'

'Exactly what I said. Now, any preference foodwise?'

Puzzled by his abruptness, she shook her head. 'I eat anything and everything.'

'You must have a good metabolism, then,' he murmured, inspecting her curves appreciatively. 'If you're happy to eat at the local pub we can go in my car and come back for yours. And I can recommend the food.' He appeared to have forgotten their difference of opinion completely.

'That's fine by me.' As they made their way across the car park she became increasingly aware of his masculinity, and wished that she'd made her escape as she'd intended. She was already allowing him to cross the boundary she'd drawn to protect herself from being hurt in the future.

The moment they walked into the bar of the Swan a man of about the same age as the doctor came forward to greet him.

'Hi, Ross. Your usual table?' Without waiting for an answer he led the way to a corner table beside a roaring log fire.

Ross McKava was obviously a *very* regular customer. Did that mean his house was permanently empty of a home-maker? Reminding herself that his private life was nothing to do with her, Beth heard him introduce her. 'Mike, this is our new practice nurse, Bethany. We've overworked her on her first day so I'm making amends.'

Beth flushed, sure that he was making the point for her benefit that there was nothing more to it.

'Pleased to meet you, Bethany.' Mike extended a welcoming hand.

'Beth, please,' she told him, trying to release her hand from his lingering hold.

'You know how to pick 'em, don't you, Ross?'

The doctor appeared irritated by the remark. 'I had nothing to do with choosing this one, unfortunately. I was delayed by a heart case so only met her this morning.'

Beth was left with the firm impression that even had he not been delayed she would have been his last choice.

'Where's the menu, then, Mike?'

As the other man hurried away to collect it from the bar Ross said, 'Mike Gurdon's the owner and, I warn you, he doesn't need any encouragement.'

Beth's eyes widened with disbelief. 'Encouragement? I only asked him to use the name everyone else knows me by.' She knew he hadn't missed the fact that her cheeks were flaring with colour and wondered if he believed that it gave the lie to her denial.

'Fine. I just wanted you to know what to expect.'

What did he think she was—a raving nymphomaniac?

Without a word she took the menu that Mike held out to her and decided quickly that she'd like the dish of the day.

After ordering the food at the bar Ross returned with the elderflower cordial, diluted with sparkling water, which she asked for, together with a weak shandy for himself.

She watched him as he settled back into the capacious Windsor chair, and, despite her determination to shun future relationships, her heart gave an uncontrollable flip, as it had done that morning. He really was incredibly handsome and was made even more attractive by his amusement at her close inspection. It showed not only in his dark eyes but also in the teasing curve of his lips.

Steepling his fingers together, he said, 'Who did you *really* think I was this morning?'

The heat that had been slowly subsiding from her cheeks returned, stronger than ever. 'An intruder, like I said.'

'How did you think I got in?'

She shrugged. 'I didn't have time to go into the logistics of it! My one thought was to stop you rooting through the confidential records.'

'Why? What value did you think they were to

me? Surely a genuine intruder would be looking for drugs, or money, or something he could sell?'

'I wouldn't know. I don't mix with the criminal classes.' Anger at his amused probing was making her say things she didn't mean. She supposed that she *had* been stupid, but that was looking at the situation with hindsight. At the time she had imagined the only partner she hadn't met to be much older, so what else could he have been but an intruder?

'So what did you think I was doing there?'

If nothing else she had to admire his persistence! 'All right, you asked for it. I thought you were a cardboard-box-dweller who'd been released from a psychiatric hospital!'

CHAPTER THREE

INSTEAD of giving the angry outburst Beth expected Ross roared with laughter. 'I suppose I did look as if I'd slept rough,' he agreed when he finally regained control of himself. 'But didn't it occur to you that I might just be a doctor who'd been up all night?'

'Well, no.' She didn't relish the thought of telling him why, but recognised that he was someone who would not rest until he got the truth, and the whole truth at that. 'You were the only member of the practice I didn't know and I thought. . .' Her voice tailed off.

'Ye-es?' he prompted, leaning forward so as not to miss a word she said. 'You thought. . .?'

'Well, I imagined you to be nearing retirement.'

His guffaw made several of the other diners turn to look at them. 'What on earth gave you that idea?'

'I suppose I thought you weren't at my interview because you wouldn't be here much longer.' She forbore to add that it was usually the older doctors who didn't appreciate having the help of a practice nurse.

His grin wider than ever, he shook his head incredulously. 'You won't get rid of me that easily! Actually, I intended to be at the interviews, but you were a *fait accompli* by the time I could leave the emergency I'd been called to. As you well know.'

Recognising that he was talking about their chance encounter in the car park, Beth suddenly wished that she had refused his invitation, especially when he said, 'Now, you were going to tell me earlier why you don't like reps, but you didn't get a chance.'

As she was making a fresh start at a place where no one knew that her husband had been a drug rep who'd been killed on a jaunt with another woman, she tried to dismiss the subject lightly. 'It was only a joke. They have a job to do the same as everyone else. I wouldn't want to be one, though.'

He gave her a searching look which left her in no doubt that he didn't believe a word she had said, so it was a relief when the home-baked ham in cheese sauce they had ordered arrived.

'That was quick!' Suddenly realising how hungry she was, Beth tucked into the food immediately. 'Mmm—this is delicious,' she told him.

He laughed. 'You'd better not come here too often, then, or I shall be blamed for your diminishing curves!'

'Diminishing?' she exclaimed. 'Surely you mean increasing?'

He shook his head solemnly. 'No. *You'd* fill

out between the curves, I'm sure.'

His banter was obviously designed to relax her, but the watchful gaze of his dark eyes unnerved her and she didn't enjoy the meal.

'What are you expecting from this job?' he asked suddenly.

'Expecting? What do you mean? I enjoy my work and usually find it rewarding.'

He picked up on the word as she'd intended that he should. 'Usually? Does that mean you're not sure about the Windber practice?'

She met his gaze levelly. 'I haven't had much of a chance to find out so far, but I can tell you now that the way you expected me to work today is not my idea of practice nursing.'

He raised a dark eyebrow and said coolly, 'I gathered you were saying as much to Joanne earlier.'

She flushed, but if he'd already overheard that she planned to make changes she might as well tell him why. 'Dr McKava——'

'Do call me Ross,' he interrupted.

'Dr McKava,' she persisted, 'I've worked as a practice nurse for many years now and have always had my own list of patients, as well as the odd ones passed on from the doctors' consultations. In return I've asked the doctors I've worked with to see those with whom I've felt out of my depth.

'I can assure you that I have no intention of usurping your position or doing anything I'm not qualified to do, but neither am I prepared to twiddle my thumbs until you think there's a task you don't want to demean yourself with.'

She guessed that she'd gone too far, but she was tired and considered that he'd provoked her. However, she was unprepared for his retaliation.

'If your previous employers were that perfect why did you leave the job?'

Beth stared at him silently, her eyes wide with panic. Why had she been so foolishly determined to get her point of view across? If she hadn't been so tired she would have seen the danger lurking ahead. It would be stupid to throw away this chance to escape from her unhappy memories without giving the job a fair trial.

When she didn't offer an explanation, he shrugged. 'You obviously aren't prepared to tell me. In that case——' he regarded her thoughtfully '—let me tell you, I'm always open to any suggestions that might improve the way we run things, but I don't consider that you're in any position to make them until you've been with us long enough to see how things work already. And I warn you, the practice will only take any suggestion on board if we *all* agree that it'll be an improvement, so don't try to convert the others behind my back.'

'I wouldn't expect anything else,' she retorted hotly, aware that her silence had raised a suspicion in his mind.

'Well, in return I must confess that I haven't

particularly considered the view from your side of the employment contract, but that's not surprising when your predecessor didn't exactly set a good example.'

'So I'm being judged on the actions of others, am I? Is that why you referred to me as interfering *and* a women's libber this morning?'

He grinned, making her angrier than ever. 'Perhaps that *was* somewhat presumptuous of me. I have to admit that my views are coloured by the only two practice nurses I've worked with. One was so hopeless that she actually increased my workload, the other was extremely efficient but her career got in the way of everything else.'

Beth sensed a sudden bitterness in his tone and realised that her outburst could have done nothing to change his opinion. She said quietly, 'I'll try not to cause you any problems, if only because I'd hate to be put into either of those categories.'

He searched her features hopefully, then murmured, 'Only time will tell. But I must say——' he made no attempt to hide the glint of devilment in his eyes '—— you are the first one with such expressive eyes that I know what you're thinking even before you say it. That must surely be a point in your favour.' While Beth struggled to find a fitting reply, he changed the subject. 'Now, tell me where you are living.'

'Ascot Gardens.'

'Nice area. Your husband must have a good job.'

Not prepared to endure his sympathy on top of everything else, she remained silent.

'Has he not moved down here yet?'

'No—I'm living there on my own.'

'Permanently?'

Why the hell did he have to be so perceptive? She couldn't tell him an out-and-out lie. 'I'm afraid so.'

He regarded her solemnly for a moment then asked, 'Do you want coffee?'

Uncomfortably aware that his attitude of amused tolerance had changed to disapproval, she refused. 'In fact, I think I'd like to get home now. It's been a long day. But you don't have to move. I can walk back to pick up my car——'

'No way—but are you sure you don't want coffee first?'

'No, thanks.'

He pushed his chair back abruptly and, having settled the bill, silently led the way out into the car park.

Why, oh, why hadn't she curbed her impetuosity instead of trying to make her point so forcefully? She couldn't imagine what he must be thinking about her now, but his expression told her it wasn't good.

An even more awful thought possessed her as she climbed into the passenger seat. Perhaps he was now wondering if she was on the lookout for a new relationship.

She sought frantically for a way to let him know

that that was the last thing she wanted. Even though her broken heart was slowly healing she was determined never to give another man the opportunity to hurt her as Richard had done.

They were back in the surgery car park before she'd found the words she was searching for, and when Ross leaned across and opened the passenger door Beth knew that the opportunity was lost. All she could do was show her appreciation. 'Thank you very much indeed for the meal. It was great.'

'And thank you for the company,' he responded in a voice that lacked its earlier warmth. 'Drive carefully.'

She nodded her farewell and her heart thudded painfully at the thought that though she'd done her best throughout the day to prove her worth all her efforts had been negated by her refusal to talk about Richard's death and the stillbirth of her daughter that had followed.

Beth was not officially required to work Saturday morning, but she made sure that she was in her treatment-room even before Ross, who was the duty doctor, started that day's surgery for emergencies.

She had seen no patients when he came striding through to the treatment-room in search of dressings and stopped short at the sight of her.

'Good Lord, what are you doing here?'

Uncertain of his reaction to her presence, she

tried to sound confident. 'Trying to learn the routine as soon as possible so that I'll be more of a help than a hindrance.'

She released the breath she had unconsciously been holding when he nodded approvingly. 'But we don't actually need a nurse here on Saturdays. There's only ever one doctor on duty as the surgery's for emergencies only.'

'I'm aware of that, but I'm here today. If I can be any help let me know.'

He stared as if surprised by her offer, then said, 'You could dress this poor old dear's varicose ulcer for me. She's experiencing quite a lot of discomfort. She's due to see the dermatologist on Monday so we need just to tide her over the weekend.'

'What dressing?'

'Granuflex, please.'

Beth nodded. She had used hydrocolloid dressings in her last practice and they had generally been very sucessful.

She walked back to Ross's consulting-room with him and, after he'd introduced her, helped Mrs Wheeler across to her room.

'Let's get you up on the couch, then I can make a better job of the bandaging.'

Mrs Wheeler grinned wickedly. 'He said there wasn't a nurse here, but I'm glad you are. Doctors aren't any good at bandaging. It's never comfortable when he's done it!'

Beth grinned conspiratorially. 'Doctors aren't

trained to do it. They have different skills.' She completed the bandage. 'Now, have you a prescription to get?'

The elderly lady nodded.

'How did you come here today?'

'By bus—I couldn't have walked.'

'If you can wait I'll run you home when the surgery's over and we'll collect the tablets on the way.'

She helped Mrs Wheeler into the empty waiting-room and settled her comfortably, with her leg resting on a stool.

'I shouldn't be long. Would you like a cup of coffee?'

'No—I'll be running to the loo if I do.'

Beth found her a magazine to read and went back to tidy the treatment-room.

'Anybody with Dr McKava?' she asked Joanne, who was manning Reception.

The girl shook her head. 'No, I think we've seen the last of this morning's list.'

Beth knocked quietly on his door.

'Come in!'

He looked up and his smile of welcome raised Beth's hopes for an improvement in their working relationship. 'There's no one waiting for you so I thought I'd run Mrs Wheeler home.'

'You don't have to do that. She——'

'I know I don't, but I want to. I just wondered when you were going to see Mrs Cavington.'

His head lifted sharply. 'Why?'

'I'd like to go along as well. That's if you don't mind.'

'In your own time? Such dedication!'

His scathing paraphrase of her own accusation of the evening before made Beth flinch. It was the last response she had expected. Colour flaring in her cheeks, she turned to leave without a word.

However, he was on his feet and had grasped her arm before she reached the door. 'I shouldn't have said that, but I'm not used to staff volunteering for extra duties unless they have an ulterior motive.'

Beth stared at him with amazement, unwilling to believe that he could be so cynical and yet wondering what had made him that way. Shrugging her arm free, she told him coldly, 'I intended making an appointment for Mrs Cavington to see me this morning, but you'd already told Joanne to put her down for a home visit.' She glared angrily, then added, 'I've always followed up the patients I look after. As well as giving them continuity of care it makes my work more interesting. However, please forget——'

Ross interrupted her. 'As it happens I do have some paperwork to do, so if you're back before I finish you're welcome to come. In fact,' he went on with a capricious smile, 'I want to call on Kylie as well. Would you like to see how she's getting on?'

'Please don't delay yourself on my account,' she snapped, banging the door behind her. How dared he be so condescending? If he expected her to join him now he was very much mistaken.

'Right, Mrs Wheeler. Let's be going.' She helped the elderly lady out to her car.

Fate aided her determination not to be back at the surgery by the time he was ready to leave on his visits. The pharmacist she went to first had run out of the tablets on her patient's prescription so Beth had to go much further afield for them.

Then, after helping Mrs Wheeler into the house, she couldn't leave her without clearing up the chaos she found in the kitchen and making the old lady a hot drink and something to eat.

As she boiled the kettle she smiled to herself with wry satisfaction. Ross would definitely have left by now, and she had the perfect excuse if he accused her of finding something better to do.

Consequently she was surprised when she saw his car outside the surgery as she drove by on her way home. After a moment's indecision she reluctantly pulled into the car park. The last thing she wanted now was to go on the visits, but neither did she want to strain their working relationship further if, by any chance, he *was* waiting for her.

She let herself quietly into the surgery and was surprised to find him sound asleep, his long legs stretched out on the stool she had provided for Mrs Wheeler. As he caught up on the sleep he'd lost over two nights on call his exhaustion lent him an air of vulnerability that she wouldn't have believed existed.

He awoke with a start, and she thought she detected a momentary flash of pleasure in his eyes at the sight of her, but his look was immediately shuttered as he leapt to his feet, conscious of her catching him unprepared.

'Hi; I thought you'd got lost.' His usually deep and melodious voice held an edge of gruffness. He brushed an unruly strand of hair back with an impatient hand.

'I'm sorry.' She settled into the chair beside him. 'I couldn't leave poor old Mrs Wheeler in the state she was in. I had to do a bit of washing-up and organise her with a snack to keep her going until her friend comes in later this evening.'

He shook his head as if unable to believe what he was hearing. 'We have an extensive list of patients, Beth. You can't look after them all personally.'

She glared indignantly. 'I don't intend to.' She rose to her feet and collected her bag. 'I presume you've completed your visits?'

His quiet reply surprised her. 'Only a couple of local kiddies with viral infections. There's always the possibility of meningitis, so one can't be too careful, but the two rascals I saw today should be OK by Monday. Having reassured myself about that, I took the opportunity to catch up on my snooze time until you were ready to accompany me on the others.'

Surprised, Beth swallowed hard. 'I—I see. I——'

'You've changed your mind, haven't you?' he accused her, before she could finish what she was saying.

'No, of course not.' Hoping his waiting meant that he was beginning to appreciate her appointment, she continued, 'It was just that I didn't expect you still to be here.'

The moment she'd said it he shot her a veiled look that left her unsure whether he was angry with her scepticism or with himself for doubting her motives earlier.

Leading the way out of the building, he locked the surgery door behind them before saying, 'If you still want to come we can take my car and come back for yours later.'

A repeat of the previous evening was the last thing Beth wanted. 'I'd rather follow in my Fiesta if you don't mind. Then I can go straight home when we've finished.'

He seemed surprised, but didn't argue. 'OK, then; I'll see you at Mrs Cavington's first.'

Their patient of the night before seemed much happier and more comfortable. 'I've been expressing the milk the way Sister showed me,' she told them proudly. 'It's a treasure you've got there, Doctor.'

Ross was noncommittal. 'And how's baby Jason—satisfied with just one milk bar?'

'So far. He's sleeping at the moment.'

'If the pain's bearable you could put him back on the other breast tomorrow.'

Mrs Cavington seemed surprised. 'Tomorrow?'

Ross turned to Beth. 'Don't you agree?'

Startled at his seeking her opinion, she mumbled, 'The sooner the better.'

Jason's two-year-old brother gave a loud bellow. 'He's just woken up,' Mrs Cavington reassured them.

'I'll bring him down for you.' Beth spent a little time chatting to the boy before she picked him up, and he clung round her neck quite happily.

'You can take him with you if you like,' his mother joked when Beth rejoined them in the living-room.

'I don't think he'd want to leave his brother,' Beth said as she stood him down on the floor.

'I'm not so sure about that.' Mrs Cavington laughed as she showed them to the door.

They left with the happy mother's repeated thanks ringing in their ears. Ross grinned as he helped her into her Fiesta. 'One satisfied customer at least.'

'Two to be exact,' Beth joked. 'Jason *and* his mother.'

'You can remember the way to Kylie's house?' he asked, seemingly reluctant to close her door.

'Of course.'

'Are you sure you want to come? After all, the visits are my responsibility and must be eating into your plans for the weekend.' He made the suggestion tentatively, causing Beth to wonder if he was trying to discover what she got up to in her spare time.

'I don't have any—apart from catching up on too many neglected household tasks.'

'That doesn't sound much of a relaxing time.'

Hoping to make him abandon this line of conversation, she laughed. 'Oh, it will be. I find needlework very relaxing.'

'Needlework?' he queried.

'Yes. I intend making cushion covers. My new flat needs brightening up.'

'I see. In that case we'd better get on.' He closed her door and climbed into his own car.

Beth sighed with relief. She couldn't deny that she found him attractive—too attractive for someone whose trust had been so cruelly abused so recently.

He must have given her replies some thought on the journey for he was waiting for her at Kylie's gate with a puzzled frown. 'I thought you were living in that flat before we appointed you.'

Not wanting to explain that her unhappy memories had driven her from the tiny cottage in Maidenforth where she had expected to be a wife and mother, she nodded. 'I was. There's more agency work around in the large conurbations.' He couldn't read anything into that statement, she thought with satisfaction.

'So when did you move here?'

'Five weeks ago. I'd already applied for this job

so the choice of where to go was easy.'

'What if you hadn't got it?'

She shrugged. 'The agency were confident that they could keep me in work.'

'Do you need any help to get settled?' As he asked the question she noted an unusual tension in his voice.

Afraid of the sudden, intense awareness of him that washed over her, she shook her head emphatically. 'I can manage fine.' She laughed. 'There's a lot to do and I get on much faster with no one interrupting me.'

He didn't answer immediately, but rested a firm hand on her shoulder before saying, 'OK—but if you do ever need help let me know.'

He then led the way abruptly into the house and, swallowing hard, Beth guessed that she had just made another mistake where her boss was concerned. He evidently wasn't used to having his offers refused!

Kylie was much better. 'I'm writing more poetry for you,' she told Beth shyly when Ross had finished examining her.

'What's this?' Ross was curious.

'I wrote a poem about her yesterday.'

'You didn't show me.' Ross pretended disappointment.

'This is it.' She showed him the verse in her exercise book. 'Sister Beth has a copy too! She says I should write more.'

'So you should.' Ross rested his arm along her

shoulder as he read it. 'That's good. What have you done today?'

But Kylie wouldn't let him see. 'It's not finished.'

'Show me next time, then?'

She nodded, and Ross went on to say to her mother, 'I think she ought to stay in and write more rhymes today. The wind is too cold for her at this stage.'

'But. . .but, well, I must go out and get some food and I can't leave her here on her own. If I wrap her up warm?' Mrs Rennell queried anxiously.

'I'll stay until you get back, Mrs Rennell.' Having made the offer impulsively, Beth was immediately conscious of Ross's disapproval.

'Oh, thank you, Nurse, thank you.' Mrs Rennell's gratitude was excessive.

'She's a sister, Mum. It says so on her badge.'

'You *are* feeling better, Kylie,' Ross joked, ruffling her hair before turning to Beth and saying quietly, 'Are you sure you can spare the time?'

'Quite sure,' she answered quickly, knowing that he was recalling their earlier conversation.

He shrugged and she guessed that he wasn't best pleased that she could spare time for the Rennells but not him. 'In that case I'll leave you to it and see you Monday.' He still appeared reluctant to go, but eventually went at the same time as Kylie's mother, much to Beth's relief.

CHAPTER FOUR

Mrs Rennell was back before long. 'I hope I haven't held you up, Sister. I don't suppose you get much time off.'

Kylie fell asleep while they shared a pot of tea and her mother told Beth that her husband, Ken, had walked out when she'd found that he was cheating on her. 'Because he was a rep it was all too easy for him to stay away nights without me knowing any different.'

Having been through a similar experience, Beth found it easy to sympathise and she stayed much longer than she had originally intended.

As she rose to leave, Kylie stirred. 'Goodbye, Kylie. Keep on writing.'

'Can I go out tomorrow?' the little girl asked eagerly.

Beth hesitated. 'It depends how cold it is. If the wind drops, maybe, but I don't think that's very likely.'

The little girl's face dropped with disappointment.

'Did you want to go somewhere special?'

Kylie nodded. 'Our Sunday-school class is doing a bit of the service at church. They're using one of my poems.'

Beth turned to Mrs Rennell with a frown. 'Is the church near by?'

'No,' mother and daughter answered together. 'There isn't one on the estate yet,' Kylie continued. 'It's the chapel in Leek Street.'

Beth thought rapidly. When she'd moved to Windber she'd seen the chapel and meant to find out if the services were to her liking. This would be an ideal opportunity. She wouldn't have to go alone and Kylie would hear her poem.

'I'll take you if you like. What time's the service?'

'Half-past ten.' Kylie's face was wreathed in smiles.

'I'll come just after ten, then.'

'Are you sure?' Mrs Rennell asked as she showed Beth to the door. 'We don't want to impose.'

'No. I'd like to go. See you tomorrow.'

Beth found plenty to do once she arrived home. Although it was newly decorated by the landlord, there were several homely touches she wanted to add.

Unearthing her sewing machine from the back of the wardrobe, she made a set of multicoloured cushions to brighten up the drab settee and chairs. Spurred on by the effect, she made a tablecloth out of the remaining piece of material.

The Sunday morning service turned out to be a family one that lasted a bare forty minutes, so it didn't give Beth much of an idea about the normal services, but she was glad that they had gone nevertheless. Kylie was even asked to read her own poem about nature, and returned to her seat looking happier than Beth had ever seen her.

After the service, Mrs Rennell was buttonholed at the pew entrance by an older lady who chatted volubly. Kylie and Beth were trapped in the pew. 'That's my Sunday-school teacher,' Kylie whispered. 'I expect she wants to know where Dad is. He used to bring me. Mum never came till he left.'

'I see.'

'I thought Dad might be here.' Kylie looked sad again. 'But he isn't.'

Beth tried to cheer her up by changing the subject. 'Your poem was lovely—and you read so well.'

Mrs Rennell had finished her chat by that time so Beth ran them home. 'Come in for a coffee?' the older woman asked.

Beth shook her head. 'I'd better get home. I've a lot I want to do.'

Kylie looked disappointed but Mrs Rennell nodded her understanding. 'Thanks again, Sister. Kylie really enjoyed the outing.'

When she arrived at the surgery on Monday morning Beth found that Ross and Liz had surgeries starting at nine and she herself had patients booked in for her attention. She raised her eyebrows in surprise at the number of notes awaiting her, but, carrying them to the treatment-room, thumbed through and saw that they were all Liz's patients, together with one of David Murrin's. The fact that none was Ross's told her that she hadn't made any progress in eliminating his prejudices as she'd hoped.

Ah, well, Rome wasn't built in a day, she thought. She called her first patient through. It was a young girl—Teri—requiring inoculations. She was starting work soon as nanny to an American family in Grenada.

'I've come for the last in the course,' she told Beth with relief. 'Dr Harsham gave me all the others as there was no nurse here at that time.'

'It must have made a lot of work for the doctors.' Beth drew up the solution and quickly administered the injection.

'Gosh. That was the best one ever. I didn't feel it at all.'

Beth laughed. 'Doctors don't have as much practice at injections as we do. Grenada sounds wonderful. Especially on a rainy day like this. I should think you'll have a wonderful time out there.'

Teri's enthusiasm was bubbling over excitedly. 'I can't wait, although I'm going to have my hands full with a two-year-old and a new baby to look after.'

Beth cautioned her, 'I don't know if Dr Harsham warned you, but these inoculations are not infallible. It's still important to be careful about what you eat and drink. Use bottled water if at all possible and if you have to use it from a tap do boil it first or treat it with water-purification tablets. And be careful about ice in drinks—that's a common cause of tummy upsets.'

'Thanks—I must say I wouldn't have thought about the ice.'

'Don't forget to wash fruit in your purified water as well.'

'At this rate I'll be afraid to eat anything!'

Beth laughed. 'I'm not trying to make life a misery for you—rather the opposite. Tummy upsets are the pits so if they can be avoided by a few simple precautions it's worth it. And if you stay long enough to become accustomed to the bugs you'll be able to relax your guard a little. It's just common sense really.'

'I know.' Teri was slipping her jacket back on. 'Is there anything else I have to do?'

Beth checked her records. 'No. All done. When do you actually go?'

'Thursday.'

'Have fun, and take care.'

She couldn't contain her excitement. 'Thanks, Sister; I'll send the doctor a card when I'm settled.'

The door reopened to admit Ross almost immediately and a young man hopped in behind him.

'This lad's gone over on his ankle and torn his

ligaments. Could you bandage it up?'

'Certainly.' Beth helped the youth into the treatment chair and raised his leg.

'His name's Andy.' Ross hovered as she moved across the room to collect the equipment she needed. 'Which bandage will you use?'

Beth threw him a scathing glance. 'Crêpe. That's the current thinking, isn't it?'

Ross seemed surprised by her up-to-date knowledge. 'Yes—yes—it allows more movement than the adhesive strapping a lot of people still use.'

He followed her back to the patient.

'If you've got more patients I can manage,' Beth informed him curtly.

'I'm interested in watching your technique.'

Beth couldn't resist the opportunity. 'Hoping to learn something, are you? Mrs Wheeler said your bandaging wasn't up to much.'

Ross turned on his heel and left the room without a word, causing Beth immediately to regret her gibe.

Andy grinned engagingly. 'That told him, Sister.'

Already conscious of the damage that her impulsive response had done, Beth bit her lip. 'It was wrong of me to say that. Doctors are trained in different skills.'

She bandaged his leg comfortably, then asked, 'Has the doctor said to weight-bear?'

Andy nodded. 'If it's not too painful.'

Beth helped him down gently. 'Rest one hand on my shoulder while you test it. Right. How does it feel?'

'Much better, thanks. I can walk almost normally.'

Beth acknowledged his thanks. 'The more you use it the better. You know where to find me if you want it reapplied.'

'I 'spect my sister'll do that,' he told her as he left the room. 'She's a nurse at the hospital.'

The remainder of the morning sped by for Beth as a succession of patients made their way into her treatment-room. Some just needed reassurance, others were to be weighed and have their blood-pressure measured, and she easily coped with the variety of dressings, treatments and tests ordered. It was all routine work that she'd been trained for, and she loved every moment of it.

So, despite having noted the absence of Ross's patients in her list—apart from Andy—Beth was in a contented frame of mind when the senior partner appeared in the doorway and leant against the jamb, watching her finish off her paperwork.

'Have you someone else for me to see?' she asked hopefully.

He shook his head. 'I've finished my quota for the morning. I just wanted a word with you. Are you busy?'

Beth consulted her list. 'Five minutes to my next appointment.'

He closed the door. 'Mary tells me you took

Kylie and her mother to church yesterday.'

'Yes.' Beth was immediately on the defensive.

'I don't think that's a good idea—any more than your compromising your spare time by looking after Kylie while her mother goes shopping. You'll encourage her dependence on you and when you let them down Kylie will be the one to suffer, as when Mr Rennell left.'

'*When* I let them down?' she echoed furiously. 'Mrs Rennell knew it was a one-off situation. Kylie wanted to go to the special service because it used one of her verses. If I can help in my own time I don't see why I shouldn't—same as I took Mrs Wheeler home and sorted things out for her. Just because I'm a professional, does that preclude my doing good turns?'

Ross appeared startled by her spirited defence. 'Of course not. As long as you don't promise what you can't deliver.' He shrugged and, turning on his heel, left her to call her next patient through.

His effrontery took her breath away, but she guessed that it could just be that he was getting his own back for her earlier gibe, which she had been wrong to make in front of a patient. She wondered what it was about him that made her want to try and get the better of him, and it took her a couple of minutes to pull herself together.

'Mrs Wold,' she called.

The lady who came through was smartly dressed and made up. If Beth hadn't read her records she wouldn't have believed that the patient had ever had a weight problem.

After checking her blood-pressure and weighing her Beth complimented her on the continuing improvement, then asked, 'Is there anything else I can do for you?'

'Well—er—I'm not sure.'

Beth seated herself as if she had all the time in the world. Whatever Mrs Wold wanted to say she wasn't finding it easy and Beth was prepared to wait.

'I believe you took Kylie Rennell to Leek Street chapel yesterday.'

Beth blinked. Did everyone in Windber know? 'Ye-es. Is there a problem?'

'Ken Rennell's father was my brother and I brought Ken up. He's like a son to me.'

'I see.' Beth knew that she must wait until Mrs Wold was ready to tell her more before she could understand.

'The poor little girl's had a hard time.'

'Asthma is a distressing disease——'

'I'm not talking about her health—and now her mother, Carina, won't let me see her. She says I'm interfering.' She went on in a rush, 'I can't help being worried. That woman's inadequate and can't cope.'

Beth waited and, when Mrs Wold didn't go on, asked softly, 'What makes you think that?'

'Why do you think Kylie's father left? He could see how useless she was. She wouldn't listen, and gets in such a state—she makes Kylie worse.'

Aware that this was a totally different tale from the one Mrs Rennell had told, she suggested, 'Mrs Wold, I think you're perhaps being a little unfair. An asthma attack can be very frightening for the onlookers—and it's even worse if you are alone with the sufferer.'

'Are you saying it's my Ken who's to blame?' Mrs Wold was indignant. 'He'd put up with it for twelve years.'

Beth inclined her body towards her patient, wanting to make it clear to her that she wasn't taking sides but trying to get at the facts.

'I wouldn't say anyone's to blame. These things happen and we just have to find the best way of resolving the problems that result.'

'I'd like to see Kylie again, but her mother won't bring her to see me.' Beth wasn't at all sure that the tears now sparkling in Mrs Wold's eyes were genuine.

'I'm sure she will when she's able, but have you considered how difficult life is for her now? They'd only just moved out on to that estate— hadn't had a chance to make friends, had they? So, with no transport, Mrs Rennell isn't prepared to move far at the moment. Have you thought about visiting them?'

The tears miraculously dried. 'How am I going to get out there? It's way out of town and very few buses run that way as yet. . .' Mrs Wold stopped as she recognised that she was expecting

Carina and her sick child to do what she wasn't prepared to attempt herself. 'Er—well,' she blustered, 'perhaps I should give it a bit longer. After all, he's not been gone a month.'

She rose to her feet and made for the door. 'Same time next week, Sister?' she asked, as if the discussion about her great-niece had never taken place.

'That'll be fine, and keep up the good work. Another pound off next week and you'll have lost a stone since you began.'

Mrs Wold forced a smile, but it didn't reach her eyes, and she left Beth feeling strangely dissatisfied.

Had Ross been right? Was it a mistake to become too involved in her patients' lives? There was no doubt that Mrs Wold had thought so, but for what reason Beth couldn't imagine.

She shook her head and, after making notes on the patient's records, called the last person on her list through to the room.

'Mr Stock.' She returned to the treatment area to wait for him. When he didn't materialise she called him again. 'Mr Graham Stock.'

Ross came out of his room and, after speaking briefly to the receptionist, nodded to Beth. 'I've seen him for you.'

'But—but——' Beth knew that she was spluttering unbecomingly ' —he wasn't even your patient. He was David's.'

He raised a placatory hand. 'He didn't want to

wait, so, as David isn't in this morning, I saw him. It's no problem, and as it happens it was just as well that he consulted a man.'

Beth glared at him. 'He wouldn't have had to wait long.'

Ross motioned her back into the treatment-room and closed the door behind them. 'I wasn't being difficult, but the receptionist told me that you had Mrs Wold with you so I guessed it might be a long session.'

'Why?'

'I thought I'd made that clear earlier. This might be a larger place than you've been used to but it's still too small a community to interfere in people's lives.'

'In—interfere?' she stammered, but, ignoring her, he went on.

'None of us can make any move without being noticed *and* I know Mrs Wold of old. Now about Mr Stock——'

'Yes?' Beth prompted.

'He has an enlarged prostate, so you'd only have had to refer him on to one of us.' He didn't wait for a response but continued, 'So what did Mrs Wold want?'

'She came for her weekly blood-pressure and weight check.'

He raised his eyebrows sceptically, leaving Beth with the uncomfortable knowledge that he had guessed that that wasn't all there was to it. However, he changed the subject completely and asked, 'What are you doing for lunch?'

'Er—I haven't really thought about it.' She checked her watch and then her list of appointments for the afternoon to hide her indecision. 'I haven't enough time to go home, so——'

'You'd better come to the Swan, then—they do food at lunchtime.'

Distrustful of his rapid change of mood, Beth countered the suggestion. 'I've too much paperwork to catch up on, and anyway I have a cooked meal in the evening.'

'You can have just a snack. We all need to get away from the surgery for a few minutes,' he told her firmly. 'We try and go most days. Liz is probably there already.'

In that case Beth saw no harm in joining them. 'OK! Give me a moment to clear up. Do you want to put anything on Mr Stock's notes?' She held the records out to him.

'I'll just make a quick note.' He crossed to his room.

Beth was soon ready and waiting apprehensively.

'Reach you at the Swan?' Julie, the morning receptionist, asked with a knowing smile as Ross reappeared.

Ross raised a hand in acknowledgement. 'How did you guess?'

'My shout this time,' Beth insisted as they ordered at the bar. Before he could argue she handed over a twenty-pound note.

Mike, who had been watching, grinned and said, 'Met your match, Ross?'

Ross barely inclined his head in reply. Instead he led the way across to the table they'd shared on Friday evening. Aware that Mike's comment hadn't exactly pleased him, Beth looked around her. 'No sign of Liz—or David.'

He shrugged. 'Dave's been off for the weekend so he's probably got a meal for her. He doesn't have to be back until evening surgery.'

Beth was puzzled. 'You mean Dave and Liz. . .?' Not quite sure how to phrase it, she allowed her question to tail off.

Ross laughed at her delicacy. 'Didn't you know they're married? Liz uses her maiden name professionally.'

'No, I didn't know. How should I?' Feeling as if she'd been tricked into coming to lunch with him, she snapped, 'I don't know anything about you either!'

'We'd better remedy that situation. I had a long-standing relationship, which finished some time ago. And I don't want to talk about it.'

Well, that was one good thing. He should be able to accept, then, that she didn't either. She nodded her understanding as he spoke again, changing the subject. 'What made you decide to make a move?'

'I needed a change of scene.'

'Because your marriage broke up? Surely you'd have done better' to remain among friends?'

Beth sighed deeply. 'I didn't have the opportunity.'

Ross frowned, then thought he understood. 'You mean—you worked with your husband?'

She shook her head. Why, oh, why did he have to be so persistent? She just wanted to forget that part of her life.

'No. I'd already left work because I was pregnant.'

'So that was it. I couldn't understand why no reason for leaving was given in your excellent reference.' He went on to enquire accusingly, 'So who's holding the baby? Your husband?'

Beth was furious. Had he been checking up on her? What was he trying to do—catch her out? Having asked her previous employers not to say anything about Richard's death in her reference, she had hoped that they would discreetly forget her reason for leaving as well, and it seemed that they had.

She compressed her lips against her reeling emotions before muttering, 'If you must know, Richard died in a car crash just over a year ago and Naomi was stillborn a month later.'

He gave an agonised groan and leaned across to rest a comforting hand over hers. 'That was clumsy of me. I should have recognised that you weren't the type to farm out your offspring.' The sudden tenderness that invaded his eyes alarmed her and she snatched her hand away.

Surely he wasn't so ignorant of the realities of

modern life? Beth was not amused! 'Believe me, if things had turned out differently I might well have had to.'

Mike arrived with their order at that moment, but Beth was so locked into her own memories that she didn't notice immediately. '*Bon appétit.*' Mike was clearly aware of the tension but was determined to wait for a response.

'Thanks—it looks delicious.' Ross picked up a fork dismissively. Beth echoed his words and Mike left them, albeit reluctantly.

Although their exchange had left her bereft of her appetite she was determined to prevent Ross quizzing her further so quickly tried a small forkful. 'It tastes good too.'

They had both chosen vegetable lasagne, and Beth soon tasted again the reason why the Swan was such a regular haunt and resolved to enjoy her meal despite Ross's presence.

When they had both cleared their plates of every morsel and Beth had expressed her appreciation Ross asked gently, 'Do you want to tell me about your husband?'

'My husband?' She hunched her shoulders defensively. 'Why should I, any more than you want to discuss your ex-girlfriend with me?' She was conscious that she must sound petty, but she had come to Windber hoping to start afresh where no one knew what a disaster her marriage had been. Confiding in Ross would defeat that intention.

He quirked an eyebrow, but didn't pursue the subject. Instead he said, 'About Kylie. And her great-aunt.'

'Who? Oh, you mean Mrs Wold.' Beth wiped her mouth with a paper napkin, scrunched it into a ball, checked her watch and pushed her chair back before asking suspiciously, 'What about them?'

'I think we need a case conference with the whole team, including Mary.'

'Sounds like a good idea.' She nodded. 'Is Mary the only social worker attached to the practice?'

'Yes. She's good, but very busy.'

'So I noticed.' Beth checked her watch. 'There'll soon be patients waiting for me. However, I am free at four-thirtyish, so if you want to arrange something then, fine.'

He shook his head. 'I think we need everybody involved. I'll try and arrange it for Thursday lunchtime. We often have a get-together then.'

He followed her from the bar. 'I'll run you back.'

'No problem. I can walk.' Having noted the solicitous tone that had crept into his voice, she decided that the less she was alone with him the better. The last thing she needed was his sympathy suffocating her.

'And keep your patients waiting?'

She retorted, 'I can move fast when I want to.'

His face broke into an unexpected smile. 'I can

believe that. Come on. I'm going your way before I go on a couple of visits.'

They arrived back in the surgery as the afternoon receptionist came on duty. Joanne's surprise at seeing them together wasn't lost on Beth, and she determined that she would ask the receptionist more about Ross at the first opportunity, but her afternoon was busier than she had expected. It was after five when she showed her last patient out and found Helen, the part-time nurse, waiting to take over on her shift.

'How's it going? Finding your way around OK?'

Beth suddenly realised the enormity of what she'd done. 'Oh, Helen, I've changed all the cupboards around—I didn't think about you. You won't be able to find anything.'

'Never could anyway. Don't you worry about it. I hear you're even trying to get the boss under control.'

'The boss?' Beth frowned.

'Our senior partner. Surely you've realised by now that it's difficult to do anything to please him? Workwise at least.' She laughed wickedly.

Beth thought it best to say as little as possible. 'I thought it was just me.'

'You must have done something right—Joanne tells me you went to lunch together. Unheard of!' All the time she was talking Helen was rummaging through the cupboards. 'Seems a sensible arrangement. . .'

CHAPTER FIVE

PUZZLED, Beth asked, 'What's sensible?'

'The way you've arranged the cupboards. You'd better be off, hadn't you? It's way after five.'

After a confusing day, Beth found Helen's repeated change of subject exhausting. She'd wanted to ask what Helen had been hinting at when she'd said that going to lunch with Ross was unheard of, but the moment was lost. The other woman's thoughts were racing far ahead.

Before Helen could broach another topic, Beth announced, 'Right. I'll just take these notes back to Joanne. See you tomorrow.'

The receptionist grinned at her. 'Off home? On your own?'

The suggestive remarks were beginning to make Beth feel uncomfortable. 'What do you mean?'

'Nothing.' Her expression was innocent.

'Why did Helen say my going to lunch with Ross was unheard of?' she asked as she handed over the notes.

'That's just Helen's chatter. Take no notice.'

'There's more to it than that, isn't there?'

Joanne shrugged. 'These days Ross usually keeps himself to himself.'

'He told me it was usual for everyone to go to the Swan for lunch.'

'It is for the doctors.' Her meaning was clear.

'But Mike seemed to hint that I wasn't the first girl Ross had taken there.'

Joanne shook her head. 'Not recently—he used to go there regularly with his ex. Ruth, she was called. I always liked that name,' Joanne murmured thoughtfully.

'And she left just as this place was ready to move into?'

'Oh, no. It's over a year since she got a high-powered administrative job.' She paused before confiding, 'Actually we all expected him to marry Ruth. She was brilliant. Knew practically as much as the doctors and they all relied on her far too much. Ross especially. That made it all the worse when the next girl was so hopeless.'

'In what way?' Beth queried.

'You'd better ask Ross that.' Joanne gave a nervous giggle. 'I never knew the whole story but I do know that, having heard the gossip about his previous girlfriend, she lavished attention on him, which was the last thing he wanted.'

'So why did she leave?'

Joanne didn't reply but unexpectedly immersed herself in checking some notes and Beth knew why when she heard Ross's voice behind her. 'She was incompetent,' he told her shortly. 'Can I have the next notes, please, Joanne?'

As he strode back to his consulting-room Beth

knew that he was annoyed and wished she hadn't asked. She hurried to collect her jacket and leave.

She'd barely had time to switch on the oven to reheat the casserole she'd made the day before when the telephone rang. Lifting the receiver, she heard Ross's deep voice. 'Beth?'

'Yes?' Surely he wasn't phoning to reprimand her for her curiosity?

'I wonder if you'd do something for me?'

'Y-yes?' she replied tentatively, wondering what was coming.

'Kylie's bad again. I know you're off duty and it's not really your responsibility, but she knows and trusts you. Would you mind visiting her until I finish the evening surgery? Then I'll be straight over.'

'No—no, of course not.' Wondering why he didn't send Helen, she quickly turned the oven off and rushed to her car. Did this mean that he was beginning to trust her abilities after all? No, more likely it was, as he had said, because Kylie already knew her. She'd be foolish to read any-thing more into it.

When she arrived at the now familiar house on Windber Gate Estate Kylie's mother flung the door open with relief.

'Come quick, come quick. She's choking— quick, do something.'

Beth rushed into the downstairs room and, find-ing Kylie more distressed than she'd seen her before, motioned her mother to leave them to it.

'Hello, Kylie. It's me — Beth. Haven't you been using the spacer?'

The girl nodded briefly, too breathless to speak. Registering that the girl's pulse was indicative of a moderate attack, Beth guessed that it had again been made worse by her mother's anxiety. She reached for the nebuliser which Ross had left at the house and placed the mask over the girl's nose and mouth.

Kylie looked up at her with eyes wide with terror. Beth took her hand and tried to reassure her. 'Just to help your breathing settle down, love; you won't need it for long.'

She felt the girl begin to relax and her breathing become easier. Offering a silent prayer of relief, she smiled warmly at Kylie. 'What's happened to Teddy?'

Kylie reached round to her pillow and pulled out the well-worn animal.

Heavy footsteps on the path told Beth that Ross had arrived. He bounded into the room and grinned at them both. 'It doesn't look as if you need me after all.'

Beth removed the mask from the girl's face and, turning the oxygen off, waited to see if Kylie's breathing remained easier. Mrs Rennell came anxiously into the room. 'How — how is she?'

'Much better, aren't you, Kylie?' Beth stood back to allow Ross to examine the girl.

He listened to her chest carefully. 'Nothing to worry about there.'

Relieved, Mrs Rennell offered, 'Coffee?'

They both nodded gratefully. 'That'd be fine.'

While Mrs Rennell chatted to Ross in the kitchen Kylie confided to Beth, 'Nanna Wold rang. She and Mum had a row.' Tears sprang to her eyes and her breathlessness increased. 'She wants to come and see me, but Mum doesn't want her to. She says Nanna's not even Dad's mother, only his aunt.'

Beth listened with growing dismay as she recognised that this attack was her fault. She was the one who'd suggested the visit.

Ross came back into the room and again checked Kylie's chest. 'I think we can safely leave you, young lady. I want you to continue with the same regime, but you *must* use the spacer every time. OK?'

Kylie nodded and he gave her a wink. 'Just you behave yourself. Don't do anything I wouldn't do. And look after Mummy.'

Beth couldn't help smiling at the obvious rapport between doctor and patient.

When they left Ross enquired, 'Why the smile? Because I said to look after her mother?'

'I was just glad you said it. Kylie's growing up fast so the sooner she ignores her mother's fussing the better.'

'I'm pleased you agree because Kylie has become very attached to you in a short time. I've even suggested that she pop in for a chat with you when she's back at school.' A laugh rumbled in his throat as he opened her car door. 'Perhaps we should adjourn to the Swan to continue our mutual admiration.'

Beth didn't hesitate for a moment. 'No, thanks. I've a casserole waiting at home.'

'You cook as well? Unbelievable.' As their eyes locked she read in his expression a mixture of incredulity and empathy.

Embarrassed and frightened by the emotions he was capable of stirring within her, she tore her gaze away and asked raggedly, 'Wh—what do you mean, "unbelievable"?'

He shrugged. 'I suppose I saw you more as a career girl.'

'Can't I be both?' Although relieved that the dangerous moment had passed, Beth couldn't imagine where he got his outdated ideas from.

He seemed embarrassed. 'Of course you can; it's just. . .'

'Yes?' Beth prompted, but he seemed to have lost his train of thought.

'Nothing. I'm sorry I disturbed your evening.' He seemed reluctant to take his leave, however. 'You could always save the casserole for tomorrow,' he cajoled.

Beth was tempted as she climbed into her car, but, only too aware of her vulnerability, she knew she would regret it.

'No, thank you.' She sought hurriedly for an excuse that would convince not only him but herself as well. 'I—I have important letters to write.'

'In that case I'll see you Wednesday,' he told her huffily. 'I've a day off tomorrow.'

As she set off down the road Beth checked her rear-view mirror and nearly relented when she saw the look of dejection on his face. But, recalling what Joanne had told her about his reaction to the attentions of the previous nurse, she knew that she'd done the right thing.

She spent a restless night during which her feelings alternated between relief that she would not have to work with Ross the next day and a strange desolation at not seeing the one person she had spent most of her time with since joining the practice.

For she had to face it—since Friday they had been thrown together almost to the exclusion of every other member of the practice staff—a state of affairs that it would be foolish to allow to continue, especially as it was already causing her disturbed nights.

She had come to Windber to make a new life among people who knew nothing about her traumatic past, and she needed safety in numbers, not Ross's undivided company.

She resolved to try and be a little more circumspect when he next issued one of his unorthodox requests, for the signals he emitted were far too confusing. One moment he apparently distrusted not only her work but also her motivation, and the next he seemingly expected her to be

at his beck and call, whether she was on duty
or not.

Arriving at the surgery on Tuesday, she discovered that Liz and Dave had no compunction
about channelling patients in her direction. Her
full appointment book soon chased all thoughts
of the senior partner from her mind.

As the morning progressed she was pleased to
find a couple of Ross's female patients waiting to
consult her, but was not surprised to discover that
they had both had to insist on having the appointment with her rather than Ross. Apparently Julie
was a formidable disciple of her boss.

'I only need a repeat prescription of the Pill,'
the first girl told Beth, placing a specimen of urine
on the desk between them. 'I always used to see
the nurse and there was no problem, but last time
the receptionist said I had to see the doctor.'

Beth smiled reassuringly. 'I gather the practice
has had a couple of spells without a nurse. You
probably came during one of them.'

'So why did the receptionist try to put me off
seeing you today?' the girl asked petulantly.

Beth hid her own disquiet with a laugh. 'I only
started here on Friday and they haven't got used
to me yet.'

The subject was dropped as Beth started to
measure the patient's blood-pressure. 'That's fine.
Let's weigh you now.' Beth recorded her findings.
'Everything's OK. Your weight is exactly the same

as last time. I'll get Dr McKava to write out the prescription for you.'

The second patient, Tracey, was not so easy. Only sixteen, she took the seat that Beth indicated and promptly burst into tears. Beth pulled her chair closer and waited till the worst of the outburst was over, then asked gently, 'Now, what's the problem?'

'I think I'm pregnant,' Tracey sobbed brokenly.

'What makes you think that?' Beth asked quietly.

'I let my boyfriend. . .' Sniffing loudly, she couldn't continue for a moment. 'Well—we made love last week and now my period's late.' She ended the sentence in a rush, her head down.

Beth handed her a tissue from the box on the desk. 'Was that the first time?' The girl nodded, but still didn't look up. 'Did you use any protection?'

Shivering miserably, Tracey nodded again. 'I insisted he used a condom.'

Beth heaved an inward sigh of relief. That lessened the possibility, at least—*and* reduced her concern about disease.

'Are your periods usually regular?' Beth asked gently.

'Yes—well, not too regular.'

'So how far overdue are you?'

'Three days.'

'And you haven't done any tests yourself?'

'No—I've no money.'

'OK, I can do that for you tomorrow if you bring me an early morning specimen of urine. I must warn you, though, it's early days yet so we may have to repeat it. However, as you used a condom there's a good chance that you aren't pregnant, although it's certainly not impossible. Try and relax a little in the meantime. Being uptight can only too easily make your period late.'

The girl nodded. 'I know that, but I wish I'd never done it. I shouldn't have done it, should I?'

Beth got up and put a consoling arm round the now standing girl. 'It's no good torturing yourself with regrets, although if it wasn't the result of a carefully thought out decision you should perhaps think hard and long about your relationship before deciding whether to continue or not.'

The girl started hesitantly, 'B-but all my friends——'

Beth interrupted sharply, 'Never, ever allow others to influence your decision, and don't be coerced by your boyfriend either.'

Tracey said resolutely, 'I wanted to do it. At the time. I just didn't expect to feel so bad about it afterwards.'

Beth smiled gently. 'That's sad, because with the right person at the right time you should feel just the opposite. I think the way you feel is being made worse by your present uncertainty. So what we have to do now is resolve that worry, then work out ways to prevent your going through this torment again.'

'You mean go on the Pill?'

Beth sighed as she recognised that her earlier homily had apparently fallen on deaf ears. 'That's certainly one option, but let's not worry about that until we see what happens tomorrow.'

The girl managed a watery smile. 'Thanks, Sister, for being so understanding. I was terrified of telling you.'

'Tracey,' Beth reassured her quietly, 'we're here to help you, whatever your problem. You won't find us judgemental. That's not what we're here for. Please don't ever be afraid of coming here for help or advice.'

'I wouldn't be frightened of you any more, but doctors scare me stiff.'

'Why? They're only human.'

Her patient was silent for a moment. 'I know that, but, well, they're different somehow.'

Beth shook her head. 'Not really. When did you last see one?'

Tracey shrugged. 'I saw Dr McKava when I had a sore throat—when I was just starting at secondary school.'

'That long ago?' Beth grinned. 'All children feel like that. Just remember you're an adult now and you'll see things very differently.'

Rising to her feet, Tracey nodded. 'I suppose so. I'd better be going, then.' She didn't sound convinced, but Beth hoped that she'd allayed some of the girl's fears.

'I'll see you tomorrow, then. Make an appointment on the way out.'

Beth continued to see patients until lunchtime. Most required repeat treatments, checks or injections and a few were looking for advice. Although she didn't get a break during the remainder of the morning Beth experienced a quiet satisfaction that she'd done her best for each patient.

The afternoon was even busier as the baby clinic was in session. Sticking needles into the tiny limbs was perhaps the task she disliked most as a practice nurse. She coped by telling herself she was being cruel to be kind. The inoculations that she was giving would protect them from the nastier infections as they grew up.

However, her disturbed night had begun to affect her by the time Helen arrived to take over and she felt thoroughly out of sorts. When she'd handled Jason Cavington she'd congratulated herself that she'd one so without her grief at the loss of her daughter resurfacing. But she'd found a whole afternoon clinic of babies a different matter.

She was preoccupied with thoughts of a long, quiet soak in a hot bath as she left for home; consequently she didn't see Ross's car, about to pull into the parking space beside hers, until she started to reverse and he gave a blast of his horn to warn her of his presence.

After slamming on the brake she climbed from

the car, waited until he had safely parked his BMW, then asked brusquely, 'What are you doing here? I thought you had the day off.'

'Bad day?' he responded sympathetically, his eyes searching her features relentlessly.

'No. I've had a very good one actually.' Beth knew that she was being deliberately provocative. 'I was allowed to make my own decisions.'

He looked at her with a raised eyebrow. 'Meaning?'

She turned to climb into her car. 'If the cap fits!' She couldn't have explained why she was being so perverse, or why his apparent understanding was infuriating her. Unless handling all those babies had turned her hormones upside-down.

'Look, as you said, it's been a long day and you must be tired.' Placing a firm hand on her shoulder, he swung her round until she couldn't evade his searching gaze. 'Why don't you join me for something to eat later?'

Disturbed by the way his casual touch was making her want to agree, she refused emphatically. 'Not tonight, thanks.'

Gazing intently into her eyes, no doubt trying to assess the reason for her refusal, he cajoled, 'Your choice—it doesn't have to be the Swan.'

She shrank away from contact with his hand. His overt masculinity was making her stomach twist uncomfortably, and there was nothing she would have liked more than to abandon herself to his company for the evening, but she knew that it wouldn't be fair to either of them when she had nothing to offer. Marriage to Richard had seen to that. 'I have to get home, thanks.'

'I see.' He appeared to be disappointed. 'I should have realised that you might have other plans. I thought an informal chat, away from the surgery, would be a good idea. For both of us.'

All the tension of the day suddenly drained from her body as she recognised his attempt at conciliation. He must have thought himself to blame for her reluctance to join him the previous evening when, in reality, she had only refused his invitation because she couldn't trust herself. 'I'm sorry, Ross, but I really *am* tired. Too tired for conversation. Could we leave it for tonight?'

He tried unsuccessfully to hide his surprise at her refusal of his offer. 'OK. If that's what you want. We can perhaps make it another night.'

'Perhaps.'

'And perhaps not,' she muttered to herself as she climbed into her Fiesta. With a brief wave, she drove away to her empty flat and makeshift evening meal, which left her with a long evening to fill—an evening when unsettling thoughts of Ross refused to be banished from her mind.

Unable to settle to anything, she showered and went to bed early, but sleep evaded her until the early hours, when her last waking thoughts reinforced her resolve not to allow him to monopolise her time.

Ross was already in his consulting-room with a patient when she arrived next morning and, collecting her pile of notes, she was surprised to see Mrs Cavington's on the top with a scribbled message attached. 'Could you check the abscess for me? I don't want to keep her waiting.' It was signed by Ross.

Beth experienced a deep satisfaction as she read the note. He couldn't consider her completely useless at work, then.

Last night he'd offered a conciliatory chat, and now this. Surely both were good omens for the future. Perhaps her recent indifference towards him personally was allowing him to appreciate her as a professional.

'Mrs Cavington.' She called her first patient through and was delighted to see her looking much happier and baby Jason sleeping soundly in his carry-chair. 'I don't need to ask how things are.'

'Everything's nearly back to normal. The pain's gone and he's feeding well. And I'm using the pump to stop getting overfull again, like the doctor said.'

'Sounds great. Can I just check you over?' Mrs Cavington slipped off her jumper and bra, allowing Beth to examine both breasts carefully.

'There seems to be no problem now. You're not even tender today.'

Mrs Cavington shook her head. 'It's all thanks to you, Sister. I don't know what I'd have done if that receptionist had sent me away on Friday. Topped myself, I think.'

'I don't think so. And you know if I hadn't been there Dr McKava would have seen you when he had a moment.'

'I couldn't have waited to the end of the surgery.'

'You wouldn't have had to. The rules are made to be broken in cases of emergency.' Still ashamed that she herself had jumped to the wrong conclusion, she didn't want her patient to do the same.

'If you say so, but I'm still very glad you *were* there.' Mrs Cavington was dressed again now and ready to leave. 'Do you want to see me again?'

Beth thought for a moment, then decided to be safe rather than sorry. 'I know it must be difficult with your toddler, so don't make an appointment—just pop in the next time you're passing.'

Mrs Cavington nodded. 'I don't like leaving Andrew with my neighbour unless I really have to. Since Jason was born he's become difficult to control.'

Beth smiled. 'I expect his nose is a wee bit out of joint at the moment, and because you're tired it seems worse than it really is. I'm sure it'll soon pass.'

'I hope so. I really do.'

'Don't forget—let us know immediately should the problem come back.'

'I certainly will, Sister, and thanks again.'

Later in the morning another of Ross's patients consulted her about a recurrent indigestion problem. Her condition wasn't responding to over-the-counter antacid preparations, but she didn't want to trouble the doctor unnecessarily.

Beth sensed the patient's anxiety and, after questioning her gently, asked her to wait while she found out if Ross could fit her into his morning's appointment schedule.

'No problem,' Julie told her. 'A couple of patients haven't turned up so he's ahead of himself. I'll push her in next. Send her out into the waiting-room and let me have her notes.'

'I'd rather speak to Ross about her myself before he sees her.'

Julie shrugged, but agreed that she'd let Beth know when Ross was free.

He was much longer than Beth expected. She had dealt with two patients before Julie summoned her.

He seemed preoccupied when she entered his room, and she waited silently while he made copious notes, presumably about his previous patient. Eventually he looked up. 'Did you want something?'

'Yes. I'd like you to see this patient, Mrs Munden——'

'Is it important, then?' He looked pointedly at his watch.

'Well, it's an ongoing problem, but it could be serious. She's extremely anxious and, having told her that you can see her, I'm not sure if once she leaves the waiting-room she'll have the courage to come back.'

Ross sighed deeply. 'Why on earth did you say I'd see her without checking with me first? I either see her now and keep those with appointments waiting or I risk her not consulting me at all and it being my fault when it turns out to be something serious. You've put me in an impossible position.'

CHAPTER SIX

BETH gasped. 'That's a bit unfair,' she defended herself hotly. 'Before I said anything to Mrs Munden I asked Julie if you had a free appointment. She told me you were ahead of yourself as patients hadn't turned up. She didn't know any more than I did that you were going to take so long with your last patient.'

He gave a resigned sigh. 'It was pure chance that someone needing more time came when I thought I had plenty of it. It's just a pity I didn't know about Mrs Munden before I started the consultation. However, there's no point in wasting more time. Tell me about her.'

'She's had indigestion for many months—it's not helped by antacids and she's terrified because her mother died of stomach cancer——'

Having already scanned the notes Beth had made, Ross broke in impatiently, 'OK. I'll see her now.' He asked for the patient over his intercom, and, passing her in the corridor, Beth gave her a reassuring smile and went back to see the remainder of the patients on her own list.

It was lunchtime when her last patient, Tracey, came anxiously in with her specimen of urine. Beth seated her comfortably before crossing the room to carry out the pregnancy test, chatting all the while about anything she could think of apart from what she was doing.

Finally she returned to take the seat alongside Tracey. 'I'm pleased to say it's negative.' Seeing the girl visibly relax, Beth cautioned, 'We're not out of the woods yet. We need to repeat it at the end of the week. But it's a good sign that it's negative so far.'

Tracey started to cry. 'Oh, Sister, I'm so relieved. I don't know what I'd have done.'

Beth found herself spending the whole of her lunch-break counselling the girl and by the time she started her afternoon duties she felt emotionally exhausted.

Consequently, when Kylie unexpectedly came in as Beth completed her afternoon helping Dave with the diabetic clinic she greeted the girl like a long-lost friend. 'Hi! What a treat to see you here. Dr McKava did say you'd be dropping in for a chat, but I didn't expect you so soon.'

'I'm so much better that I thought you'd like to see how well I can blow out. And how well my writing's going.'

'Have you brought your meter?'

Kylie nodded and, raising the mouthpiece to her lips, blew sharply. 'That's good, isn't it?'

'Much better, Kylie.' Beth recorded the result in her daybook. 'Well done. Now, what have you been writing?'

Kylie handed over her exercise book and Beth

saw the poem, which followed the one she had a copy of. It wasn't finished but described a romantic liaison between Ross and his nurse.

'Hey, we only work together. You can't write things like that. Dr McKava might not like it.'

'It's only pretend——' the little girl laughed nervously '— because you're both so nice to me and the doctor's so good-looking.' Kylie closed the book firmly. 'I'll let you see it again when it's finished.' She clutched the book to her chest. 'It'll be our secret.'

'Is your mum with you?' Beth thought it best to change the subject.

'Yes. She wanted to see Mrs Banks about something. She's in with her now. My teacher sent me some work today, and Mum told my friends I'll probably be back at school on Monday.'

'That's good.' Secretly Beth thought that it would have been better for Kylie to go back before the end of the week, but she didn't say so. She'd caused enough trouble with her comments to Mrs Wold!

Kylie seemed to read her thoughts because she looked up, her eyes misting. 'Nanna Wold hasn't come yet.'

Beth hurriedly reassured her. 'It's not an easy journey out to Windber Gate Estate on the bus. Perhaps she'll come another day.'

Kylie nodded ruefully. 'I hope so. I wanted to go and see her now, but Mum says it's too far.'

'Quite right. You don't want to overdo it on your first day out.'

'I know, but I do want to see her again.'

Noting the tears welling up in the girl's eyes, Beth knew that Kylie was remembering the telephone row of Monday evening. She grasped a small hand comfortingly. 'You will. Maybe not immediately, but the social worker's helping your mum to work through her anger at everyone connected with your dad.'

Kylie asked tearfully, 'Will she let me see my dad soon, then?'

'I'm sure they'll be able to work something out.'

A slight sound behind her made Beth swing round. Ross was standing there listening.

'I didn't hear you come in.' She met the searching gaze of his brown eyes unwaveringly, and couldn't help wondering if he was checking up on her. Perhaps that was what his unexpected visit to the surgery the evening before had been for, rather than an attempt to get to know her better, as he had said.

His deep voice broke in on her reverie. 'I saw your mum in the corridor, Kylie, and she told me you're feeling much better.'

Kylie was smiling again, her tears forgotten. 'I must be 'cos I've hardly wheezed at all today.'

Provoked by his continued lack of trust, Beth recalled his comment about looking after his asthma patients himself and handed him her record of Kylie's peak flow measurement. 'I've had a long day, so I'll be off now and you can check *your* patient in peace.'

He seemed puzzled by her behaviour and held up a detaining hand. 'No need for that. I can see she's fine.'

Mrs Rennell came into the treatment-room at that moment. 'Isn't she doing well? I had to get some shopping and see Mary so I brought her with me. I thought you'd like to see how much better she is.'

They both spoke together. 'We do.'

Kylie laughed. 'Do you two always do everything together?'

'Kylie!' her mother admonished.

Ross grinned. 'Sister Beth's new this week. I'm just showing her the ropes.'

Kylie nodded her approval. 'Will you still be working together when I come in next week?'

Beth shook her head. 'I shouldn't think so. We both have lots of other patients to look after.' Then, seeing Kylie's crestfallen face, she added, 'But if we know when you're coming we'll see what we can do. Won't we?' she appealed to Ross.

'Oh—er—of course.'

Kylie was content with that. 'OK. See you.'

'Why on earth did you say that?' Ross demanded the moment the door closed behind Kylie and her mother. 'I warned you about breaking promises and letting her down.'

Beth shook her head in despair. 'Just what did I promise?' When he didn't answer she went on,

'All I said was that we would see what we could do.'

'And by next week she'll have twisted that to expect me to be here.'

She shrugged. 'Well, you did say you wanted to check the asthmatic patients yourself.'

The troubled look that crossed his face told Beth that her barb had hit home, and she expected him to retaliate. Instead, he said quietly, 'I know that's what I said. I'm sorry if my way of working causes you a problem.' He turned sharply on his heel.

'Did you come in for anything special?' she asked coldly. 'Or were you just checking that I wasn't usurping your position?'

He suddenly recalled that he did have another reason. 'I'd like you to syringe a young fellow's ears. He's flying to the Far East tomorrow and I can't see the drums for wax.'

Instead of leaving her to it he roamed around the room, checking the equipment she was gathering. 'You don't use the metal syringe, then?'

'No—there's less risk of damage with this automatic machine. It provides a constant pressure of water, unlike the old-fashioned ear syringe.'

'I'm pleased to see you keep up to date. So many nurses think that once they've finished their training that's it.'

Unsure if it was a compliment or another covert criticism, she muttered, 'Another of your generalisations, Dr McKava? If you're busy I can manage. I would hate you to keep your next appointment waiting.'

He left abruptly and Beth felt a small swell of triumph as she called the young man that Ross had spoken of through to the treatment-room.

There was no one else waiting when she had finished and she quickly tidied the room. Sure now that Ross *was* still trying to keep tabs on her work, she was ready to leave the moment Helen arrived.

'I've run out of reading matter so I want to get to the library before it closes,' Beth explained. 'I expect they've got a list of what's going on in the area as well.'

Helen nodded. 'They have. But you won't see it tonight. Our library closes all day Wednesday.'

Beth couldn't believe her luck. It seemed that everything was against her. With nothing to do but watch the most appalling television programmes she had ever seen, her resentment against life and Ross in particular simmered throughout the evening.

As she walked through to the treatment-room on Thursday morning Ross called from his consulting-room, 'Good morning, Beth.'

She continued walking as she replied casually, 'Hi! It's fine at least.'

'We'll meet up at lunchtime, then,' he called after her, coming out into the corridor.

Her mind obsessed with the necessity to keep her distance from him, she decided otherwise. 'I'm going home for lunch today. Things to do, you know.'

He raised a quizzical eyebrow. 'I thought you agreed to join our conference about Kylie.'

Beth covered her mouth with her fingers as she realised her mistake. He wasn't asking her out. 'Of course. It's Thursday, isn't it? OK. I'll be there.'

'We order sandwiches in. Tell Julie your preference.' Turning on his heel, he walked briskly back to his own room, leaving Beth feeling as if she'd been through a wringer.

The morning flew by with more patients than on previous days. Ross sent several patients through to her, but she was conscious of him frequently monitoring her standard of work.

It was almost too much when he asked her to put a couple of stitches into a cut on the forearm of one of his male patients and then queried, 'Which sutures will you use?'

'The same as I always do,' she told him curtly.

'Which is?' He wasn't to be deflected.

'Four O Ethilon.'

'What would you use if it was on the face?'

'Five O.'

''Ere, you're not practising on me, are you?' the patient asked doubtfully.

Ross laughed and shook his head. 'Sister's no doubt done this many times before, but as she's new to this practice I'm just checking she uses the sutures I prefer.'

He stayed to watch her insert the first stitch, then, satisfied, left her to it, much to Beth's relief. She felt all fingers and thumbs when anyone watched her, let alone someone as critical as Ross.

Although lunchtime was fast approaching, Beth had just made herself her first cup of coffee of the morning and settled to some paperwork when, bubbling over with happiness, Tracey burst into the room unannounced.

'I had to let you know, Sister. I'm not pregnant. I started bleeding this morning.'

'That's great, Tracey. The negative test yesterday probably stopped you worrying and did the trick.'

The girl nodded and went to leave, but Beth placed a detaining hand on her arm. 'Not so fast. We need to discuss what you plan to do in the future.'

The girl took a seat. 'Can you give me the Pill?' she asked nervously.

Aware that her long session with Tracey the day before hadn't altered the girl's decision to continue the relationship, Beth shook her head. 'The doctor has to prescribe that and he'll want to see you first.'

Tracey's bubble of happiness burst immediately. 'I can't see him. He'll tell my mum and she'll kill me.'

'Tracey, you are sixteen and can make up your

own mind. Doctors take an oath of confiden-
tiality, you know. Dr McKava will not tell anyone
else unless you give your permission.'

'Are you sure?'

'Absolutely certain.' However, recalling Ross's
reaction to her request for him to see an extra
patient the day before, Beth was now torn. There
was no way she could say that Tracey needed
treatment urgently, but it would be safest if the
girl started the Pill on the first day of her period.

In the end she decided that Tracey's welfare
was more important, and said, 'I don't suppose
he'll be able to see you right away, but I'm sure
you'll be seen as quickly as he can manage. I've
made a note of what's happened in your notes,
so there should be no problem.' Showing Tracey
back into the waiting-room, Beth asked Julie if
she could find a slot for Ross to see the girl.

Shaking her head at Beth's temerity, Julie
grinned. 'I only hope he considers it as important
as you do.'

'So do I,' Beth muttered fervently, handing
over the notes. 'I've told her it might be
some time.'

The moment Beth had shown her last patient
out Ross stormed in, his face furious. 'Why on
earth didn't you let me know about Tracey
before this?'

She stared at him in amazement. 'Because there
was nothing to be done until we knew one way
or the other.'

'Nothing to be done!' he spluttered. 'You've no right to deal with something like this without letting me know. Suppose she had been pregnant and the baby had developed in one of her tubes? If she'd consulted me with abdominal pain I wouldn't have had the necessary information to make me suspect it was an ectopic pregnancy.'

Beth shook her head. 'You're being unreasonable. I recorded it in her notes.'

'That solves everything, does it? What if I'd been called out in the night and had no notes with me?'

'She has a tongue in her head.'

'That's not the point—I should have known.'

Beth drew in her breath sharply. She considered that he was going over the top, so, although conceding silently that he might just have a smidgeon of right on his side, she attacked rather then defended.

'The problem is that I never know whether to bother you or not. I was even in two minds whether to wreck your scheduled appointments today by asking you to see her, although I knew it would save her needing to take other precautions if she started her course of contraceptive pills immediately.'

'Of course it was right for me to see her today—but it would have been better yesterday. She might have listened to advice about her sexual behaviour then. It's too late today.'

'Dr McKava, over the past two days Tracey and I have discussed the subject minutely—probably in much greater detail than you would ever have time for. Whether it's had any effect we'll never know, but I can assure you I gave it my best.'

His expression almost slipped into a smile as he reluctantly admitted, 'From what she told me you made a great impression on her.' Any trace of a smile disappeared as fast as it had come. 'But that's not the point.'

'I think it is. I consider that type of consultation to be what I'm employed for and, unless ordered otherwise, will continue in the same way.'

He seemed about to say something more, then, meeting her unwavering gaze head-on, decided against it. She would never know if he had been about to bawl her out further or say she'd done well, but one thing she was certain of—a struggle was taking place within him, although Beth found it impossible to identify the varying emotions flickering there.

Reason seemed to win as he put a placatory arm around her and muttered something unintelligible before striding back across to the small conference-room where the lunchtime meeting was to be held.

Beth grinned to herself, sensing that she was slowly breaking down some of his prejudices. She returned to her room and, with a grimace, threw her cold coffee down the sink before making her way into the meeting-room where everyone else was waiting.

The only vacant seat was opposite Ross and the moment she sat down she was uncomfortably aware of his searching gaze lingering on her face.

It was a relief when Mary started the ball rolling, taking his attention. 'Kylie has improved beyond recognition over the past few days. She appears to be taking control of her illness and refusing to accept her mother's smothering to anything like the same degree.'

'I think we've all seen a difference,' Ross agreed. 'And I think most of it's down to our new practice nurse.'

Five pairs of eyes swung towards a disbelieving Beth, causing colour to flood her cheeks.

'*I* th—think i-it's due to our combined efforts,' she managed to stammer out. 'Mary's helped Kylie's mother to see a way out of the mire she's in, and Ross has given them both the confidence to cope with the bad attacks.'

'And you've encouraged her in her new interest,' he persisted. 'Personally I'd say encouraging her to write poetry is the single most important event in that girl's life.'

Beth felt even more discomfited. Had just standing up to him brought about this change? Certainly this was the first time he had given any indication that he thought so highly of her work. 'I didn't encourage her. She was already writing.'

'But you didn't laugh at her efforts either.'

Embarrassed by his unexpected acclamation, Beth shrugged dismissively.

She was relieved to hear Mary speaking again. 'I think Kylie is missing her father dreadfully, but so far her mother is refusing access. So we must just help her to accept the situation for the moment.'

'That doesn't seem fair,' Beth burst out. 'She thinks the world of her father.'

Mary nodded. 'I agree. But I think we need to take one step at a time. Rather than upset everybody by trying to get visits enforced, we're hoping to arrange conciliation counselling.'

Beth recognised that her outburst had perhaps been out of order and so kept quiet for the remainder of the discussion, allowing others to make the decision to leave things as they were for the moment and see how Kylie got on back at school.

A couple of patients with terminal illnesses were then brought forward for discussion, and, not knowing them, Beth listened in silence.

'Anything else anybody wants to bring up?' Laura asked.

'Yes.' Ross looked across to his colleagues. 'I wonder if we're expecting our practice nurse to do too much.'

The practice manager looked puzzled. 'She has the same job description as the previous nurses.' She turned to Beth. 'Do you feel overworked?'

Beth started to shake her head, but Ross didn't

give her a chance to answer. 'I didn't mean it that way. I just wondered if we're asking her to take on responsibilities she isn't trained for.'

Laura was frowning. 'What do you mean, Ross?'

He shrugged. 'Do you feel we're expecting you to cope with things you'd rather not, Beth?'

You're certainly not, she thought, searching his features for some indication of the answer he was expecting. Julie came in with the sandwiches and coffee at that moment so she was spared from having to answer immediately, but her thoughts roved wildly. Ross was certainly a complex creature—one minute complimenting, the next questioning her competence; she felt her emotions being torn apart by this man who didn't appear to know himself what he wanted of her.

When they were all settled again Laura repeated his question. Beth took the easy way out. 'I really haven't been here long enough to answer that. I've had no problem so far.'

'In that case we'll wait and see how things go.' Ross got up to leave the room. 'I've got rather a lot of visits today, so I must away.'

Beth saw a look of relief pass between Dave and Liz and guessed that Ross had been so unhappy about the previous nurse's standard of work that he had insisted that they deal with most things themselves. They obviously didn't want to return to that situation.

'As our midwife's away, can you help me with

the postnatals, Beth, or are you too busy?' Liz
was on her feet.

'I think Joanne's blocked out some of my time
to assist.'

'If you could do the blood-pressures and take
any necessary blood it would be a great help.'

'That's fine,' Beth reassured her. 'I'm sure that
won't be beyond my capabilities,' she joked.

Liz followed her into the treatment-room.
'Don't take what Ross said to heart. He's been
like this since a broken relationship. She was the
nurse at the time and I admit she was excellent,
but he won't give anyone else a chance.'

Beth nodded. 'I gathered that.'

'And the reason he's reluctant to let go of
the reins?'

Beth frowned. 'What do you mean?'

'We left his ex's successor to carry on as Ruth
always had. The problem was that she wasn't as
competent and she dealt with things that should
have been referred to one of us.'

'I think I'm beginning to see——'

'That wasn't the worst—she told one of Ross's
patients to stop making such a fuss over a viral
illness when in reality she had an ectopic
pregnancy.'

Beginning to understand the senior partner's
attitude earlier that morning, Beth gave a gasp of
horror. 'Whatever happened?'

'The patient's condition was critical by the time
she allowed her family to contact us again. Ross

forbade us to allow the nurse to take even the smallest responsibility after that.'

'I should think so too. He must have been nearly out of his mind with worry. What happened to the patient?'

'She survived, but it was touch-and-go.'

Beth shook her head. 'Well, I can assure you I probably err the other way and refer things I *could* possibly deal with, but I'd rather be safe than sorry.'

Liz nodded ruefully. 'Dave and I can see that, but it's going to take longer for Ross. After all, he could have been struck off the professional register over the incident.'

Beth murmured, 'I'm glad you've told me. I won't give the poor chap such a hard time in future.'

Liz gave her a warm smile. 'I didn't think anyone had put you in the picture.'

'Not about that horrific incident. But Joanne left me in no doubt that Ruth was so perfect that no nurse would ever match up to her as far as Ross is concerned.' Beth laughed uneasily. 'If she hadn't I doubt if I'd still be here. She made me determined to stay and prove him wrong!'

CHAPTER SEVEN

THE first time she saw Ross on Friday morning was when he brought his last patient, Mrs Wellburn, through to have her wrist splints reapplied.

'You did them so well last week,' the patient told her, 'that the pain is much less.'

'I don't think I can take credit for that,' Beth laughed.

Ross, who had stayed in the room, intervened. 'I don't know about that. It's important that they're applied correctly.'

Unsure whether he was uttering empty words to boost the patient's confidence, Beth turned to look at Ross. The smiling approval she read in his features made her uneasy, especially when Mrs Wellburn left and he stayed behind.

'Any plans for the weekend?'

Beth was relieved that she had an excuse not to accept any suggestion that they might meet. 'I'm visiting my parents.'

'On the farm?'

Beth looked at him in amazement. 'How did you know I lived on a farm?'

'Mrs Cavington told me when you were upstairs with her toddler.'

'Why on earth did she tell you that?' Beth frowned.

'Oh, she was singing your praises. Saying how unbelievably gentle you were when you expressed the milk.'

'I see.'

'Where is the farm?'

'Larbeth.'

'Larbeth? Near Gloucester?' Ross threw back his head and roared with laughter. 'If that isn't a coincidence I don't know what is.'

'What do you mean, "coincidence"?' Beth asked uneasily.

'I was born at Whitestone, towards the Welsh border.'

'Is your father a farmer, then?'

'Oh, no, he's a retired army man—into his eighties now. Mum's younger than he is, though.' He grinned. 'How about us adjourning to the Swan for an early lunch? We must surely have some mutual acquaintances to talk about.'

Wary that any further social contact might lead to the kind of involvement she wanted to avoid, she turned her back on him. 'I'll miss out on food today,' she mumbled. 'I've a lot to do before I get away and Mum will have a meal ready this evening.'

She sensed his puzzlement at her refusal as he replied, 'You'll work better on a full stomach.'

He came up behind her and, placing his hands on her shoulders, spun her round to face him, forcing her to meet his gaze. 'Don't you agree?'

When she didn't answer immediately his dark eyes searched her face with an intensity that made her recall him saying that her eyes gave away everything she was thinking. She turned her head sharply.

'What are you frightened of, Beth?' Using just one finger, he pulled her head round, no doubt to try and read the answer.

'What do you mean? I was thinking about. . .' she sought frantically for a subject to take his attention from her '. . .about Kylie.'

'Kylie? Mmm. What about her?' His eyes were smiling as he waited to see what she could possibly come up with.

'You didn't see these the other day.' She hurried across to her desk and lifted a couple of papers.

'More poetry?' he asked with smooth amusement.

Colour flared in Beth's cheeks as she recalled the poem that the child had shown her a couple of days before. 'Her peak flow measurements from the beginning of the week. I didn't know she'd brought them until she had gone.' A streak of devilment urged her to continue, 'It's a pity the early morning readings spoil an otherwise consistent pattern.'

He immediately became businesslike. 'Why on

earth didn't you say this before? I thought you would have known that early morning dips in the levels are dangerous.'

Aware that she'd got the better of him, Beth gave a teasing grin. 'Of course I know that. The morning reading on both Tuesday and Wednesday is actually higher than for the rest of the day.'

Ross didn't answer as he scrutinised the chart but closed the treatment-room door with a backward kick, causing Beth to regret her behaviour immediately. She should have kept her mouth shut. She'd made a fool of him and he wasn't going to let her get away with it.

Waiting for the outburst she was sure would come, she moved behind her desk and pretended to sort some papers. She was startled to hear Ross laughing, and laughing so loudly that she was more than thankful that he'd closed the door.

'You've been waiting all week to get your own back on me, haven't you? And you did it beautifully.' He reached across the desk and took hold of both her hands. 'OK. I give in. I have to concede that you know nearly as much as I do about these asthmatic patients so I should have known you would have let me know immediately if her levels were dangerous.'

His touch was doing untold damage to her resolve. Unable to release her hands, she raised her eyes to plead, 'Ross, please. I have work to do.'

'It's lunchtime and I don't like eating alone.'

'I've already told you, I don't have time for lunch today.'

He made no attempt to loosen his hold, but, pulling a chair up behind him with his leg, seated himself on the opposite side of the desk. 'And I asked you what you're scared of.'

Unable to escape the burning gaze of his dark eyes, she murmured, 'Nothing. I keep telling you. I have a lot to do. Now, let me get on with it.'

A tantalising trace of an expensive aftershave wafted towards her nostrils as he raised her hand to his lips and brushed it lightly with a kiss. Startled, Beth was about to enquire what he thought he was doing when her hand was released.

He clambered slowly to his feet, watching her all the time. 'All right. If that's what you *really* want.'

As she watched him leave she was tempted to run after him and tell him that it was the last thing she wanted. But deep down she knew she was doing the right thing.

She hardly stopped for a moment over the weekend. She accompanied her mother and aunt on a shopping expedition on Saturday morning, and then joined her father out in the fields as he checked his crops.

On Sunday morning the whole family attended morning service at the local church. But, despite her manic activity, Beth no longer felt a part of the Larbeth community and, to make matters worse, her enjoyment of the whole weekend was marred by a desolation that gnawed at the pit of her stomach.

Her unconscious search for the security that had been so cruelly snatched away from her made her eager to return as soon as possible to the routine of her life at Windber.

As she drove back there on the Sunday evening she was contentedly considering the week ahead when her thoughts were interrupted by an uneven noise from the passenger side of her car. Pulling into a convenient lay-by which overlooked the Windber reservoir, she saw that she had a puncture.

She had jacked up the car and was lifting the offending wheel from its axle when a car stopped behind her.

'I thought it was you. Can I help?' It was Ross, smartly dressed in light trousers topped by a blue short-sleeved shirt which looked suspiciously like silk.

'I can manage.' She lifted the spare wheel on to the axle and applied the nuts loosely.

He shook his head ruefully. 'I should have realised that a career woman like you wouldn't need help with something so trivial as a puncture.'

Recognising that his deliberate provocation hid a bruised ego at her not requiring his assistance, Beth released the jack sharply and snapped, 'Will you stop categorising me? I merely thought that it would be a pity to dirty your clothes.'

'Didn't you have a good weekend?' He had followed her round to the back of the car as she stowed away the tools that she had been using.

His obvious solicitude made her defensive. 'It was great, thanks. Lovely to be back home. Mum and Dad waited on me hand and foot.'

'Home? I would have expected someone as independent as you to consider Windber your home.'

Beth slammed down the boot lid. 'Not yet. Maidenforth was once, but not any more.'

'So why did you leave?'

'You wouldn't understand.'

He turned her towards him and, without releasing his hold on her shoulders, gave her a long and puzzled look. 'Beth, am I missing something here? You said your husband died?'

She remained silent, determined not to reveal her shame at Richard's straying only months after they were married.

Ross tried again. 'Isn't it time you consigned the memory of your husband to the past and started to live again?'

'That's what I came to Windber to do.'

'But you're not doing it.'

She retorted indignantly, 'No, because you won't let me. Every time we meet you bring up the subject of my husband.' She blinked to prevent the threatening tears from spilling over on to her cheek.

'Beth——' he sighed deeply, wiping a stray tear

gently with his thumb '—consigning him to the past doesn't mean not talking about him. Everyone we come into contact with influences our future lives in some way.'

You can say that again, Beth thought bitterly, and pretended to concentrate her attention on the dirt on her hands before saying derisively, 'Anyway, thanks for the psychoanalysis, Ross. I'm sorry I can't stay to finish the session but I must get on home.'

He raised her chin with a finger and shook his head in despair. 'Try and let go, Beth, for your own sake.' Then, instead of releasing her, he tightened his hold, pulling her towards him, and before she realised his intention he leant forward and kissed her lightly. When she didn't respond he lifted his head and searched her eyes again before repeating the movement—this time with a kiss that was anything but light.

As his tongue forced apart her lips and tried to provoke a response Beth panicked and used all her strength to push him away. 'Please, Ross.' Unable now to prevent the tears spilling on to her cheeks, she brushed at them angrily as she climbed into the driver's seat of her Fiesta and slammed the door.

He called through the open window, 'I'll follow you home if you like, just in case you have any more trouble with that wheel.'

'I'll be all right.' Although sorely tempted not to, Beth stuck to her earlier resolve. 'I'm just

tired and need to be alone. I'll see you at work
tomorrow.'

As she drove she watched him following in her
rear-view mirror, but when she turned into Ascot
Road he carried on, much to her relief.

On Monday morning Beth was early into work,
despite a night of little sleep. Her insomnia had
not been due to her outrage at Ross's behaviour,
but rather to the fact that she had been angry
with herself. She had allowed him to stir emotions
that she had deliberately buried deep inside, and
what made it worse was the knowledge that all
he felt for her was sympathy—a state of affairs
that made the thought of facing him again
unbearable.

So she was more than pleased to discover her
appointment times fully booked until midday,
allowing her to concentrate on her work and shut
out all other thoughts.

The morning flew by in a flurry of dressings
and injections. However, the last patient of the
morning gave her cause for concern. Mrs Wilkes,
one of Ross's patients, had demanded to see Beth
when she hadn't been able to get an immediate
appointment with the doctor.

She was distinctly unwell and finding breathing
difficult. Beth thought at first that she was an
asthmatic, but both Mrs Wilkes and her previous
notes denied the diagnosis.

As Beth helped her on to the couch and placed

an oxygen mask over the patient's mouth and nose she asked the duration of the present illness. When she could speak Mrs Wilkes pulled the plastic mask aside. 'I had a cold last week. And colds always go to me chest.'

Beth helped her to replace the mask and settled her in a sitting position. 'Now that your breathing is easier I'm going across the corridor to find Dr McKava.'

'He's dealing with his letters,' his secretary told her. 'I should wait until he's finished. He hates being disturbed mid-thought.'

Beth would have been more than happy to delay confronting him, but she knew Mrs Wilkes could not wait. She tapped on the door and entered at his call, placing Mrs Wilkes' notes in front of him. 'Problem?' he asked, lifting his head and watching her closely.

Unwilling to meet his eyes, Beth nodded. 'She had no appointment so asked to see me. She's extremely unwell. I suspected asthma but there's no history. I'm administering oxygen and she seems less distressed already.'

Ross thumbed through the notes quickly. 'Hmm. A smoker with a history of severe childhood eczema and repeated bronchitic attacks. I'll come through and see her now.'

Beth watched as he gently questioned the patient and examined her thoroughly. 'Everything all right at home?'

The patient nodded. 'And work?'

This time Mrs Wilkes shook her head depairingly and, removing the oxygen mask, gasped, 'Too much to do.'

Ross murmured. 'That fits. I think this is another bout of your usual bronchitis, Mrs Wilkes, and it's not helped by the stress, or by your smoking.

'I'm going to start you on antibiotics as usual, but this time you also need some steroids. I'll get Sister to give you the first dose now and we'll get the rest from the chemist.'

The patient nodded as Ross continued, 'No work for the next few days. And stop smoking immediately.'

'I—I haven't—couldn't,' she gasped.

'Good. Now, how did you get here?'

'Drove.'

'Are you all right to get home?' Mrs Wilkes nodded wearily. 'OK. I'll call round to check on you later. Take your time. No rush to leave.' He turned to Beth. 'Could you take a sample for a full blood count before she goes?'

Beth smiled her acquiescence before asking the patient, 'Would you like a cup of tea, or a cold drink with the tablets?'

'A glass of water, please.'

Ross returned with the tablets, and she took them without looking at him before handing them to Mrs Wilkes with the water.

'Stay there as long as you like,' Beth told her. 'I'll just get on with some paperwork.'

The next time she checked on her patient Beth found her sound asleep, her breathing much easier. Satisfied, she continued to work quietly in the room. The rest would do Mrs Wilkes good.

Ross came to see if she was going to the pub for lunch and, relieved that she didn't have to search for an excuse, Beth shook her head and gestured silently towards the sleeping patient. He withdrew and shut the door quietly behind him.

When it was nearly two Mrs Wilkes woke. 'Oh, I'm sorry, Sister. Am I holding you up?'

Beth shook her head. 'There's no one waiting to see me at the moment.'

'Even so, I think I'll get myself off home.'

Beth helped her down and out to her car. 'You're sure you're OK?'

'Yes, I feel a lot better already.'

'Good. Dr McKava will pop round later to check the improvement's continuing.'

Ross had gone straight from the pub on his visits, so Beth hoped to avoid him altogether for the rest of the day. However, she was still in the treatment-room when he arrived for evening surgery and, not hearing his approach, was startled by his deep voice asking, 'Busy afternoon?'

She kept her head down over her books to hide the flush that rushed unbidden to her cheeks at his interest. 'It was. I had several smears to do. Otherwise I'm finding my way around the paperwork.'

He nodded approvingly. 'I've just left Mrs Wilkes. She's much better.'

Beth murmured, 'Thanks for letting me know.'

'I'd be pretty mean not to as she came to you first and you handled her so well.'

Although reassured by his praise Beth was finding conversation difficult. 'All I did was give her oxygen.'

'And reassurance—the confident way you handle these people is half the battle.'

Surprised and slightly suspicious that the reason for his sudden approval of her actions was again more that he felt sorry for her than that he thought she was doing well, Beth said, 'I appreciate your saying so, but your input is essential. I haven't had a doctor's training and I did jump to the wrong conclusion that she was an asthmatic.'

'I might have done the same myself if you hadn't told me there was no history of it. In fact, I still wouldn't be surprised if she turns out to be a late-onset asthmatic. It's difficult to judge at this stage.'

'I have to confess that I wouldn't have thought of that.'

'Thank goodness I'm not out of a job yet! And, talking about reassuring anxious patients, gastroscopy has shown that Mrs Munden has a stomach ulcer, nothing worse. Just freeing her from the worry should help the ulcer to heal, but we'll treat it with the usual medication anyway. She's so grateful that you didn't just send her away.'

She couldn't help wondering if he'd adopted that teasing tone because he found it difficult to know what to say to her. She tried to change the subject. 'What about Mrs Wilkes' prescription? Has she anyone to take it to the chemist?'

'I took the tablets to her myself.'

Beth frowned. 'I could have done that on my way home.'

He gave her a long, silent stare. 'We can't expect you to do everything. You've more than enough on your plate already.' The look in his eyes that accompanied the words was so intense that when he rested a reassuring hand on her shoulder her skin, despite her uniform, felt branded with the heat. She stammered, 'I—I prefer to keep busy.' She wanted to tell him to stop treating her like a convalescent patient but she didn't know how to handle the feelings he was generating within her.

He too seemed disturbed by the electricity passing between them as he muttered, 'It's time you were off home. By the way, have you got that puncture seen to?'

Beth nodded. 'I'm just going to pick it up.'

'Good.' He seemed satisfied. 'See you tomorrow, then.'

Beth watched him call his first patient with a mixture of exasperation and admiration. Did he think that she couldn't cope with a few extra tasks? Or did he think that she would cut corners if she took on too much? That was probably much nearer the truth, she told herself with a wry grin.

The next couple of days passed with Beth feeling like a specimen under observation. Ross seemed to be watching her every move, making working with him increasingly difficult.

By Wednesday afternoon his solicitude had reduced her to such a state of tension that she felt ready to snap. However, Kylie's timely appearance on her way home from school brought things back into perspective. 'How's it going?'

'Great. I soon caught up with my school work. Don't know what they can have been doing while I've been off! We forgot to make an appointment, so while Mum does some shopping I thought I'd see if you were here.'

Beth was pleased to see the girl and even happier when she checked the peak flow readings. 'You're doing really well,' she praised.

'I used not to bother checking my levels before I used my inhalers, but that chart you gave me makes it easy. I do most things at the right time now. Is the doctor here?'

'I'm afraid not, Kylie. We weren't expecting you and he has a long list of home visits to do. However, I'll tell him how well you're doing and I know he'll be delighted.'

'Shall I come again next Wednesday?'

'If you can. Make a definite appointment on the way out and I'll let him know. If all's well then perhaps we can leave two weeks before your next visit.'

The girl wrinkled her nose. 'It doesn't matter. I like coming to see you.'

She was about to leave the room when she confided solemnly, 'I haven't seen Dad yet, or his aunt. I hope Mrs Banks can arrange it before long.'

'I'm sure she will, but it can't be easy. And she has lots of other families on her books. However, I'll be seeing her tomorrow so I'll remind her if you like.'

Kylie nodded. 'OK. See you.' She banged the door carelessly behind her and Beth grinned to herself, wondering at the change in the girl in such a short time.

Beth was one of the first in to Thursday's lunch-time case conference. Mary updated the arrangements she was making for conciliation, and Beth reported that Kylie had been in to see her after school the day before.

'She seems to have good control of the illness herself for the first time. Her peak flow results yesterday were a vast improvement on just a week ago.'

'As I said last week, you've done wonders, Beth,' Ross told her warmly.

Unused to hearing him say anything in favour of practice nurses in recent months, the other members of the practice were startled into silence. Then he unexpectedly announced, 'Beth has suggested setting up an asthma-management clinic. Perhaps Kylie could be her first patient.' His pro-

prietorial pride left Beth feeling extremely
uncomfortable, coming as it did on top of his
earlier compliment.

'What would you do?' Liz at least seemed
interested.

'Check inhaler technique, write up with them
an agreed self-management plan, including drug
and inhaler dosage, discuss the management with
relatives, and the need to avoid allergens like the
house-dust mite. Then make regular appointments to check their peak flow records.'

'What about smokers?'

'I'd encourage them to stop and, if it appeared
that their work might be to blame, suggest a
change of job. Obviously neither of these is going
to be easy.'

The practice manager had a more practical
problem. 'When were you thinking of holding it?
It'll be a job to fit it into our schedule. Especially
if you need a doctor there.'

Beth flushed. 'It was only a vague suggestion.
I hadn't given any thought to the details.'

Laura raised an eyebrow as if to say that she
might have known, leaving Beth wondering
if Ross had deliberately made the suggestion
without giving her a chance to formulate any
concrete plans.

CHAPTER EIGHT

Ross immediately proved that he wasn't trying to make Beth look a fool by coming to her aid. 'I thought we could do a trial run with Kylie, making her appointments during the normal surgery hours.'

'Sounds like a good idea. Let's give it a try.' Liz was always eager to agree to anything that reduced her workload.

'All right by you, Beth?' Ross asked.

'Fine. I've already started Kylie on her charts.'

'I saw you'd done that!' Ross grinned proudly.

Well, really! Beth thought. She might almost have been his special protégée, when, to start with, he hadn't even been in favour of her appointment.

'Anything else to discuss today?' Laura looked at the three doctors in turn and, when they all shook their heads, said, 'Right. Back to the paperwork. Perhaps we can talk about your ideas some time, Beth?'

Beth nodded, eager to co-operate.

The group broke up quickly then—David to start his visits and Liz her postnatals. No wonder Laura had looked so exasperated. There seemed to be a clinic of some kind every afternoon.

Ross followed Beth back to the treatment-room. 'Have you seen anything more of Mrs Cavington?'

'Not so far, but she'd soon be back if it flared up, I'm sure. And she said she'd pop in for a final check when it's convenient, but it's not really necessary. I just thought she'd be happier.'

'Are you busy at the moment?'

Beth checked her diary. 'I'm supposed to be helping Liz with the postnatals if the midwife's not available.'

'Do you want to come and see how Mrs Wilkes is today?'

'Well, yes, I'd like to, but——'

'I'll speak to Liz, then.'

He was back in a moment. 'All arranged. I told her I think Mrs Wilkes is your next candidate for the clinic so you might as well start her off as you mean to go on.'

'I see.' Beth wished that she didn't feel as if she was being manipulated. Neither of the others had suggested that she go with them on visits, and she could have found plenty to do at the surgery. But his reasoning was so plausible that she didn't see how she could refuse.

Taking the quickest route through the town centre, Ross said, 'If her breathing's easier we'll show her how to measure her peak flow today, and take it from there.'

Beth nodded. 'You think it's asthma rather than chronic obstructive airways disease?'

He shrugged. 'Only her response to treatment will tell. Her blood test result is inconclusive.'

Their patient was in fact very much better than when Beth had seen her, but she was still wheezing. Ross took a more detailed history of her symptoms than he had managed on his previous visits, and Beth showed her how to blow into the flowmeter and note down the result.

'We want you to do this every four hours— apart from the middle of the night, but the early morning one is the most essential.'

Mrs Wilkes nodded her understanding.

'You'll need to come for regular checks with Sister when you're out and about again.' Ross had picked up his bag and was making for the door, Beth in tow, when the latter had a sudden thought.

'You won't start smoking again, will you? If it's difficult let me know and I'll be glad to help.'

'I don't think I'll need any. I was so frightened by this attack that I've made up my mind I've smoked my last.'

'That's good, but you might feel differently when you're better. Anyway, you know where we are if you need us.'

Mrs Wilkes showed them out and on the drive back to the surgery Ross remarked on how sensible she was being. 'So many of my patients aren't; I feel like saying I can do nothing more until they co-operate.'

Beth didn't answer. Instead her mind was pre-occupied with what she should do if he suggested that they eat together that evening when she knew he had the evening off.

But it turned out to be wasted effort. When they got back to the surgery he didn't get out of the car but, thanking her again for her help, said, 'Take care and don't work too hard. I'll see you tomorrow. I haven't a surgery this evening,' and drove off.

After his behaviour of the past few days, to say that she felt let down would have been an understatement, and yet, she told herself, surely it was what she wanted?

It was at that moment that she realised that, if she was honest with herself, it wasn't what she wanted at all, but what she should have been grateful for! Because, after only two weeks of working together, he'd permeated her emotional awareness to a point where he could easily have broken that part of her heart which wasn't yet fully healed—a situation she attributed to Ross being an even more overwhelmingly vital male than Richard had ever been.

Friday morning was quiet, so, as lunch-time approached, Beth decided to slip home for a sandwich. She was just telling Julie where she was off to when Mrs Cavington came in with both her children asleep in the double buggy.

'Is it convenient, Sister?'

'Of course. Come straight in. It's good to see you. Everything all right?'

'Fine, Sister, fine. The breast's back to normal and Jason is feeding well.'

'I'll just give it a final check over.'

After Beth had pronounced her fighting fit again Mrs Cavington said, 'I still can't thank you enough for all you did.'

'I was glad to be able to help. It makes my job worthwhile.'

'Er—can I ask you something else or are you in a hurry to rush off?' her patient asked hesitantly. 'You were just going out, weren't you?'

Sensing that Mrs Cavington wanted to talk about another problem and wasn't finding it easy, Beth suggested, 'It wasn't important. I could make us both a cup of coffee if you'd like to join me?'

'That'd be lovely. I don't seem to have stopped this morning.'

'Let's hope they both stay asleep for the moment, then.'

Mrs Cavington's face crumpled. 'That's what I wanted to ask you about. Andrew's acting up something dreadful at the moment and I don't know what to do.'

Beth looked towards the pushchair and frowned. 'In what way?'

'He's refusing to talk and eat today.'

Beth crossed to the pushchair and rested a hand

on his forehead. It was burning. The child stirred
and Beth murmured soothingly, 'Hello, Andrew.
Does your head hurt?' The toddler stared at her
silently and unwaveringly.

'How long's he been like this?' she asked his
mother.

'Well, he's been sulking on and off for the past
couple of weeks, some days doing everything he
can to annoy me and other days refusing to do
anything I ask. Like today.'

Beth frowned. 'I think he might be unwell
today. He feels quite hot.'

Mrs Cavington frowned. 'I did wonder if he
had a virus, but it's been going on so long I should
have thought he'd be over it by now.'

Beth wasn't so sure. She opened the blinds to
let more daylight into the room, which made
Andrew screw up his eyes and turn away. She
quickly reclosed the blinds.

'Has he drunk anything today?'

'Nothing. I brought that orange juice in case
he changed his mind, but he hasn't touched it.'
She gestured towards a child's feeding-mug in
her bag.

Beth took up the mug and, kneeling by the
pushchair, slid an arm under Andrew's shoulders
and offered him a sip. He turned his head away.
Gently she tried to move his chin towards his
chest, causing him to cry out—the first sound
she'd heard from him.

'All right, Andrew. I won't do it again.' She

lifted his jumper and searched vainly for any signs of a rash.

'I think I'd like Dr McKava to take a look at him.'

'Do you think it's something serious?' Mrs Cavington was beginning to panic.

'Not necessarily. I'd just rather make sure. Here's your coffee. I'll be back in a minute.'

Beth closed the door behind her and anxiously asked Julie, 'Is Ross around?' She shook her head. Any other of the doctors?'

'No—they've all gone off to the Swan.'

'Can you contact Ross and ask him to come back to the surgery immediately? I think Andrew might have meningitis.'

She returned to the treatment-room and smiled reassuringly at Mrs Cavington, who was now agitated.

'What do you think's wrong, Sister? It *is* something serious, isn't it?'

'I'll leave the doctor to decide. In the meantime I'll keep an eye on Andrew while I drink my coffee.'

Jason woke at that moment and Beth murmured a prayer of thanks that he would keep his mother occupied for the moment. 'You see to the baby. You can pull the curtain across for privacy.'

She checked on Andrew again and, finding him even less responsive, wished Ross would hurry.

The sound of his voice asking if she was in the treatment-room was a welcome relief. He opened the door quietly and, without waiting for detailed explanations, carefully examined the boy.

Resting a hand reassuringly on Beth's shoulder, he muttered, 'Let's get him to hospital. Wrap him in a blanket while I sort things out.'

He turned to the boy's mother and told her gently, 'Andrew needs to be seen at the hospital. There's just a chance that he has meningitis.'

As Ross went out to telephone Beth put an arm round Mrs Cavington's shoulders. 'Take it easy, love. We'll soon have him in the best place and, if it is meningitis, once treatment starts he should respond quickly. I'm just going to wrap him in a blanket ready for the journey. Do you want to come with us?'

Unable to speak, the boy's mother nodded anxiously.

Ross came back and took Andrew from Beth's arms. 'The ambulance will be here any minute. They've got a bed for him at Windber General. Can you follow in your car with Mrs Cavington and Jason, Beth?' She nodded as an ambulance drew up outside. 'See you at the hospital,' he called over his shoulder.

Beth helped Mrs Cavington to load the buggy before settling her in the back seat of the car with Jason in her arms. We should be there soon after the ambulance,' she reassured her.

'Will—will he die?' Mrs Cavington was finding it difficult to voice her fears.

'We've caught it early enough for him to

respond to treatment.' Beth made the statement carefully, knowing that she couldn't give a definite answer either way. 'Does your husband work locally?'

'He's in the machine shop at Dempners.'

'When we get to the hospital I'll ring and see if he can join us there.'

By the time Beth had parked her car and they had found the ward that Andrew had been taken to he was in a cot, already attached to a drip, and preparations were taking place to take a sample of his spinal fluid so that the doctors could discover which bugs were causing the problem.

Taking the baby, Beth left his mother with Andrew and went in search of a telephone. She heard hurrying footsteps behind her but didn't take much notice until she heard Ross's deep voice call, 'Where are you off to, Beth?'

'To try and contact Mr Cavington.'

He nodded approvingly. 'And what are you going to do with the baby?'

'I'll stay here until the father arrives, then he and Mrs Cavington can decide between them.'

He grinned. 'Taking the problems of the world and his wife on your shoulders again, are you?'

Angrily she snapped, 'What do you suggest, then?'

'When Mr Cavington arrives we'll get a doorkey to enable us to collect the baby's equipment and then take him back to my house. If necessary, his mother will have to express her milk and we'll bottle-feed him.'

Beth's eyes widened with amazement, then she laughed. 'You're a bigger softie than I am. I was going to let them decide between themselves which one stayed with Andrew and which looked after the baby. I'm down to help with the ante-natals this afternoon.'

'When you've telephoned Mr Cavington I'll ring Julie and see if she can get Helen in to deal with those. We need to contact the community phys-ician as well—about preventative medication for contacts, including us.'

Beth grimaced. 'Do we have to?'

Ross nodded as he quirked an eyebrow in con-firmation. 'When Andrew was examined at the hospital there were signs of a meningococcal rash erupting. They're treating it as that until they get a result from the laboratory.'

By the time Mr Cavington arrived Ross had arranged cover for both their clinics that day, and the family had started on prophylactic antibiotics.

Ross handed Beth a pharmacy pack. 'Two days' supply for us as well. Just in case. Now we'll collect Jason's bits and pieces and take him back to my house. Hand him over while you drive.

Beth was hesitant—to go to Ross's house for the first time as a notional family unit would put her under a greater strain than she felt she could endure. 'Aren't there any other relatives who can take the baby? Grandma or aunts?'

Ross sighed deeply. 'They all live too far away. The break-up of the extended family is, in this case, one of the tragic results of our present economy. When Mr Cavington could find no work in his home town he "got on his bike" and they now live two hundred miles away from the rest of their family.

'Mrs Cavington's mother is travelling down here tomorrow. Until then we're in charge. If you drive to the surgery first we can exchange cars. Mine has more room for all the bits and pieces.'

Outside the Cavingtons' house he opened the rear door so that Beth could climb out with the baby and said, 'Let's see what we can find.'

Beth was so agitated that she couldn't think clearly about what they might need to care for Jason overnight. If Ross hadn't been there she'd have come away without most of the essentials, but he seemed to know exactly what would be needed and where to find it.

She helped him carry it all out to the car. 'You've done well. I should think you've found most things.'

'Mrs Cavington gave me a list and precise details of where things are.'

Beth felt outmanoeuvred once again. If she refused to have anything to do with his plan and left him to care for the baby himself he might see it as a dereliction of duty. If she stayed it meant them spending the night under the same roof, which to Beth seemed an even worse scenario,

especially when she thought of his recent solicitude.

'I'll go to your flat first so that you can pack
an overnight bag.' Ross's statement broke in on
her wildly tumbling thoughts.

If she offered to look after Jason there, she had
only the one bedroom, so if Ross wanted to stay
and help it would seem like an open invitation.
At least in his house there would surely be another
room she could use? She said awkwardly,
'Thanks. It won't take me a moment.'

He pulled up at her gate, and after handing the
baby to him she sped inside, pushed clean undies
into an overnight bag, then sprinted out to take
the baby again.

'That was quick.' Moments later he was pulling
the car into the drive of a large house only two
streets away from Ascot Gardens.

'I didn't know you lived so close,' Beth gasped.

He shrugged as he climbed from the car. 'Doctors usually find it better to keep their home
address private.'

Though she could see a good reason for it where
patients were concerned, she took his omission to
tell her as a sure indication that he didn't really
trust her.

He took the baby from her arms and she
climbed out. This time Jason woke and started
screaming loudly. 'I'll take everything in and then
pop back to the hospital. Hopefully Mrs
Cavington will have expressed his next feed by

now. I asked the ward sister if she could find a pump.'

He dumped all the baby's paraphernalia in what was obviously his dining-room, and, literally leaving her holding the baby, set off back to the car. 'See you soon.'

Beth followed him to the door. 'But I don't know where anything is — I——'

'Make youself at home; you'll soon find your way around.' He was gone before she could protest.

To calm her inner tumult Beth first removed Jason's very dirty nappy, replaced it with a disposable one and then, placing him in his carry-seat, set off in search of somewhere to sluice the original.

The baby gurgled happily as they made the exploration together. The first door she pushed open revealed an ultra-modern kitchen that looked as if it was rarely used. She crossed to a door opposite and was relieved to find a utility-room with an adjacent toilet that could be reached from the house or the garden.

Having dealt with the nappy, she placed it in the washing machine to wait until there were more to be washed and set off to explore the remainder of the house, putting a kettle on to boil as she recrossed the kitchen.

The living-room demonstrated exactly what Ross had said about the entire place — that it was a house but not a home. The furniture was expensive and well cared for, but there wasn't one item to indicate the hand of ownership—the atmosphere of the room was as sterile as that of a showroom window.

Remembering the clutter in the dining-room, she guessed that that must be the room he used, although even that could have done with a few homely touches to make it really comfortable.

Before she set off upstairs Beth located a downstairs cloakroom and a study, complete with computer. 'I wouldn't mind having a go with that, Jason,' she chattered to the baby as she climbed the stairs. Besides a spacious bathroom, with the biggest bath she'd ever seen, she discovered three rooms with little in them apart from beds, and one which she guessed must be Ross's bedroom.

'This is definitely the master's bedroom, Jason.' Here a feminine hand had certainly been at work. The matching curtains and king-size duvet cover were of the palest ivory trimmed with an antique lace. The toning wallpaper was lightly patterned with a pale peach floral design that was echoed on the lampshades.

Feeling like an intruder, Beth quickly closed the door and returned downstairs. She placed the carry-seat on the kitchen floor and, retrieving her overnight bag from the dining-room, took it upstairs and put it in the bedroom furthest away from the one used by Ross.

As she returned to the kitchen she heard his

key in the lock. Searching out a couple of mugs, she made them both coffee.

'Jason certainly looks happier.' He took the mug she offered. 'That's welcome.'

He placed the milk he had brought for the baby in the fridge and sat down at the kitchen table. 'I think we'll feed him on demand. He certainly looks contented enough at the moment. His mum says he'll probably want a feed about five and again at nine or ten. I'll have to make another trip to the hospital later to collect the morning feed. Thank goodness Mrs Cavington has such a good milk supply.'

'Let's hope the worry doesn't affect it. How is Andrew?'

Ross answered thoughtfully, 'Not much change, but at least he doesn't seem any worse. Thanks to you.'

'I was just in the right place at the right time,' she demurred.

'*And* you did the right thing. It's lucky for the Cavingtons that you bothered to check up on him. If he survives it'll be because you did.'

'*If* he survives?' Beth enquired anxiously.

'He's got about an eighty per cent chance with the treatment he's getting, but there's always a risk at this stage.'

She nodded. 'I suppose I knew that really. It just seems so—well, unfair really.'

'Life is unfair, love. And if we dare to think otherwise it's then that Mother Nature swings into

action to let us know we're not in control. As you
know only too well.' He pulled his chair round
so that he could put an arm round her shoulder.
'I'm sorry, Beth; I didn't think when I took your
help for granted. Is looking after the baby
upsetting you?'

Here's your chance, she told herself. Say yes
and get right away. But she couldn't leave him to
cope on his own, could she? Or was it that she
was enjoying the make-believe role of wife and
mother far too much?

Admitting to herself that her decision was not
totally unselfish, she assured him, 'No. That's no
problem. I've had to come to terms with handling
the babies at the surgery. I'm actually enjoying it.'

He turned her towards him, his gaze sweeping
her features for confirmation that she was telling
the truth. He must have liked what he read there
for he lowered his head and kissed her gently on
the lips. 'Good on you, girl,' he murmured into
her hair as he gently folded her into his arms. 'I
thought I read you right the first time I met you.'

She pulled away from him to demand huskily,
'How was that?'

'That you're a genuine earth mother who would
protect her young with her life. There's no way
that you would farm out your offspring to a child-
minder.'

She moved abruptly away from him then. 'Well,
I can tell you something, Ross—you read me
wrong. I'd have had to if things had worked

out differently. Get into the real world, for goodness' sake.'

'Be-eth. . .' He uttered her name as a long-drawn-out grumble and in the process disturbed Jason, who started to whimper. She seized the opportunity to lift the baby from the carry-seat. Nursing him in her arms would give her protection against any further advances from Ross.

He leaned across to peer at Jason's face. 'Do you think he's hungry?'

'Not particularly. I expect he's missing his mum. And dad, of course,' she added hastily.

Ross grimaced wryly. 'Dads have no option. They have to go hunting for food, or at least earn an honest crust. That's why it's important for mothers always to be at home for the children.'

Beth tried, but didn't succeed, to hide an involuntary grin. He certainly took every opportunity to ram home his opinion on the subject. 'I wish you luck in finding a girl who measures up to your expectations.'

He treated her to a lingering look that seemed to penetrate deep into her subconscious. 'I thought I had.'

Unwilling to acknowledge his meaning, Beth asked, 'You mean—well—your ex-girlfriend?' His concentrated stare was beginning to make her uneasy.

'No. I suppose I hoped she would change her views if we married, but, to give her her due, she never said she would.'

'And you couldn't accept it when she refused to do what you thought was right?'

Ross inclined his head thoughtfully. 'I suppose you could say that.'

Beth had a sudden inspiration. If she let him think she held similar views he'd take his search for perfection elsewhere. 'You should have been a Victorian. Then women had no option but to be a dutiful wife and mother. These days, when we're free to pursue whatever career we fancy, housekeeping and parenting should be shared equally. How you can expect anyone who's had a fulfilling career to be satisfied with housework I can't imagine.'

Maddeningly, he grinned as if not believing a word she'd said. 'We'll see. In the meantime, what shall we eat tonight?'

CHAPTER NINE

STILL trying to work out what he meant by that 'We'll see', Beth didn't answer immediately, and Ross must have assumed her silence indicated that she thought he expected her to cook for he added hastily, 'It'll have to be a take-away. I don't keep any food in because I eat out most of the time.' He wasn't telling her anything that she hadn't worked out for herself. 'What's your poison? Chinese, Indian, pizza or even good old British fish and chips?'

'I told you before, I eat anything and everything. You choose. Whichever is easiest.'

'OK. We can get a pizza delivered. Save me going out until I do the hospital run.'

He brought out a menu. 'More decisions. Which topping?'

By the time they had worked out a mutually agreeable choice Beth was feeling quite hungry. 'I've just realised, I missed lunch altogether. What about you?'

'Judging by last Friday, I thought you made a habit of it,' he joked. '*I* managed to get about halfway through my haddock *au gratin* before you dragged me away.'

'I'm sorry. It sounds delicious.'

'It was. I would have been very annoyed if it hadn't been urgent when I got there.' Beth knew by his tone that he was teasing. 'As it was I'll forgive you on condition that you join me at the Swan one lunchtime soon to sample it for yourself!'

'I can't wait.' She made the rejoinder in the same amused tone and didn't for a moment take his invitation seriously. 'What do you say, Jason?' She smiled down at the baby she was cradling to let him know he wasn't forgotten.

'So, if we're both so hungry, shall we order the largest size pizza, with coleslaw?'

She nodded. 'And cheesy garlic bread?'

Her pleading tone made him laugh heartily. 'If you promise to eat it all yourself.'

'I promise.'

As he telephoned the order she laughed inwardly. If that was what he wanted she needn't worry about keeping her distance from him. He wouldn't want her anywhere near!

Jason decided that he wasn't going to be left out if there was food around, so while Ross set out the utensils on the kitchen table Beth fed the baby.

'Which room do you think he should sleep in?' Ross asked as he drew the cork from a bottle of red wine.

'I put my bag in the back bedroom,' Beth told him hastily. 'We can put his cot in there, then I'll be near him if he wakes.'

Ross raised a quizzical eyebrow. 'Did you expect me to pressurise you to do otherwise?'

Miffed that he'd read her thoughts so accurately, she mumbled, 'No, not really. I just thought I'd put it out of the way.'

He shrugged. 'I'll make sure the radiator's turned up in there, then, and find some bedding for you.'

He retrieved the carry-cot from the dining-room and carried it upstairs. 'Thank goodness the Cavingtons have one of these for when they make the long journey home.'

By the time her bed was made up and Jason settled it was nearly time for their food to arrive. Ross indicated that Beth should take a comfortable seat in the dining-room and brought in the wine and two glasses.

'Cheers. Here's to us good Samaritans! Although I must say I'm quite enjoying it. What about you?'

She was saved from answering by the ring of the doorbell. Ross took their order through to the kitchen and she carried the glasses and wine back again.

He carefully helped them each to two slices of the pizza, and put the coleslaw and garlic bread in the centre of the kitchen table. She took a bite from one piece of the garlic bread.

'Mmm. It's delicious. I'm going to enjoy having this all to myself,' she told him wickedly.

To her consternation he shook his head. 'Now

I've seen it I think I'll change my mind. You don't object, do you?' She couldn't, and pushed the plate towards him. 'I hadn't really thought about it before, but it should make the atmosphere more agreeable if we've both overdosed on the garlic,' he laughed. 'Though what Jason will make of it I dread to think.'

'I'll keep my mouth firmly closed when I feed him and perhaps he won't notice.'

Ross was immediately serious. 'When *you* feed him? Surely it's my turn next?'

Beth's eyes narrowed suspiciously. 'I thought that was the last thing you'd want to do.'

'Because I said the mother's place is in the home? I'm not a total chauvinist, you know.'

Floundering as she tried to make sense of this man who was capable of playing such havoc with her emotions, she decided that the best form of defence was attack. 'You can feed him, then, and I'll go to the hospital and collect the milk from his mother.'

He vetoed that idea immediately. '*I* will go after I've fed him. I'm probably upsetting your feminist sensibilities but I wouldn't be happy to send you out to the hospital at that time of night unless it was a dire emergency.'

Feeling the colour flood her cheeks, she shook her head before saying quietly, 'You're not at all. I appreciate your consideration.'

'Well, well, well,' he mocked. 'We can actually agree on one point. There's hope for us yet.

Now, how about some more pizza?'

Having said that she was hungry, she didn't like to refuse, but she was already finding eating in his company difficult. She dreaded the direction that his conversation might take next.

But she needn't have worried. He turned to the subject of holidays, and after listening to tales of his various destinations she was able to add a few of her own.

They lingered so long over the food and wine that when Jason started screaming both were surprised to discover that it was feed-time again.

Beth left Ross to it and cleared up the kitchen. She kept waiting for him to ask for help but he managed perfectly. When he'd finished he handed Jason to her. 'You can cuddle him for a while, then when I get back I think we'll all turn in. What do you say?'

Beth agreed. Not only was she emotionally exhausted but she would feel safer once shut away in her own bedroom. She was seeing Ross in far too an attractive light.

She'd tried to impress on herself the fact that they were in an unreal situation and that tomorrow they would just be colleagues again, but her emotions didn't want to listen. The sooner she was out of temptation's way the better.

While Ross was out Jason fell into a deep sleep, so Beth carried him up to his cot and made herself ready for bed so that she could escape the moment Ross returned.

As soon as she heard the front door open she dashed downstairs. 'I've used the bathroom,' she told him nervously, 'but I couldn't go to bed until I knew how Andrew is.'

Without a word he carried the milk through to the kitchen. She followed him, waiting for an answer. He turned and swept her up into his arms. 'If anything there's a slight improvement. We must celebrate.' He kissed her resoundingly. 'We're a good team.' He was exhilarated by his news and, she couldn't help but notice, even more excited by her proximity.

'Mmm! I recognise that smell. It's Ysatis, isn't it?' He pulled her more firmly towards him before kissing her again. 'That was a thank-you for all you've done today. Beyond the call of duty.'

The unexpected physical contact aroused such a storm of sensation in her consciousness that it was all she could do not to return his kiss with interest.

He must have recognised that she wasn't completely unwilling for he enveloped her even tighter in his arms and, probing her mouth gently with his tongue, caressed the sensitive inner part of her lips, stirring up the feelings that she was trying so hard to pretend didn't exist.

However, when his hands began to move down her body she struggled to release herself from his hold. Eventually, easing her away from him, he looked down at her and asked, 'Why, Beth, why?'

She murmured hopelessly, 'This is all wrong, Ross. Just because we're thrown together in this situation. . .'

He groaned and, shaking his head despairingly, caught hold of her hand to prevent her moving away. 'Don't say it's wrong, Beth. It's the opportunity we need.'

When she didn't immediately answer he continued, 'I know I didn't exactly welcome you at first, but you have no idea how the previous nurse plagued me with attention, even offering to work nights and weekends with me. When you said that first night that your husband wouldn't be joining you I feared a repetition. I couldn't have been more wrong.'

The tenderness in his dark eyes as he spoke left her breathless. 'Despite me recognising that fact, you didn't want to know, and all the time you were proving yourself professionally too.'

In an attempt to defuse the situation she teased gently, 'As long as I only obey orders!'

He enfolded her in his arms again. 'You don't need me to tell you what to do in *these* circumstances, do you?' Holding her against him with one large hand, he moved the other up to caress the nape of her neck and she knew that if she didn't resist now she never would.

Struggling to escape, she murmured, 'I'm sorry, Ross. I must have drunk too much wine. . .'

He found her lips unerringly and silenced her opposition with a succession of kisses, but for

Beth the moment was lost as memories of Richard's infidelity destroyed her ability to trust him. She pulled away, shaking her head. 'It's no good, Ross. And I—I'm tired.' Aware of his attempts to hide his arousal, she dropped a kiss of consolation on his cheek. 'Goodnight, Ross. And thank you.'

Finally accepting that she really meant what she said, he reluctantly released her and accompanied her upstairs. He gave her a chaste goodnight kiss before uttering briefly, 'Sleep well.'

Trying not to think about what she was missing, Beth closed her door, checked on Jason and then climbed into the strange bed to try and sleep. But her jumbled emotions kept oblivion at bay, until, utterly exhausted, she fell into a deep doze. Even then, the nightmarish dream in which she learned that her baby was dead recurred with a vivid intensity that she had thought was at last diminishing.

She started awake, and, terrified, leapt from the bed to check that Jason was still breathing.

Her relief on discovering that he was, combined with the traumatic dream, caused her to break into a frenzy of sobbing. Having refused to indulge herself with open grief when she'd learnt that her baby was dead, she was suddenly aware of a sense of peace flooding over her. But still the tears kept coming as she lay in bed, trying to stifle the sobs.

There was a quiet tap on her door. 'Beth, are you all right?' She knew she must look a sight, so, holding her breath, she ignored Ross's enquiry. 'Beth?' He tapped louder. 'What's the matter? Can I come in?'

When she still didn't answer she heard the door slowly opening and in the next moment her shivering, sobbing body was gently lifted into his arms.

'I'm taking you back to my room to talk,' he whispered. 'Then we won't disturb Jason.'

Beth tried to resist but Ross was too strong, especially when a sympathetic shoulder to cry on was what she'd yearned for most at the time of losing Naomi. And since. And Ross's was the most sympathetic she'd come across!

'You'll be warmer in here.' He wrapped her in his duvet and, seating himself on the bed, cradled her to him as if she were Jason needing comforting.

'I'm s-sorry,' she sobbed, trying desperately to control her shuddering.

'Don't be,' he crooned softly in her ear. 'It's what you need.' He mopped her tears gently with tissues from the bedside table, and when the worst of her tumult was over he laid her back on the pillows and, leaning over, watched her quietly.

In the pale light from the peach-shaded lamps she saw desire lighting his dark eyes and knew without a doubt that, however much she tried to suppress it, it must be mirrored in her own. As he bent to kiss her gently her heart began to pound and thud against her ribs, snatching away her breath.

Sure that she would suffocate, she gasped involuntarily, and Ross took it as an invitation. Her reason deserting her as his sensuous caresses became more and more intimate, Beth responded eagerly, raising a storm of emotions within them both.

He lifted himself back from her and gently brushed away the tears that lingered on her cheek. 'You're beautiful, Beth, and I want you. But not this way. I won't take advantage of your distress,' he whispered.

'But Ross. . .I think I want you to.' Suddenly she needed desperately to know that someone found her attractive enough to make love to. Even if it *was* just for one night.

'Beth, darling, you said yourself that this is neither the right time nor place.' Despite his words his hands slid down to encircle the tips of her firmly engorged breasts.

A cross between a gurgle and a moan of pleasure escaped from her throat as he freed her from the restrictions of her satin teddy and lowered his lips to each pink rosebud in turn.

Jason's angry cry startled them both back to reality. Beth struggled to free herself but Ross covered her gently with the duvet. 'I'll go, love. Keep the bed warm.'

She lowered herself back on to the pillows and luxuriated in the comforting warmth of bedlinen that held the unmistakable scent of his masculinity, tinged with that subtle aftershave he always used.

Jason was soon quietened so Beth relaxed contentedly against the pillow, expecting Ross back at any moment.

The next thing she was aware of was bright sunlight invading her eyes. Stretching lazily, she tried to work out where she was, aware that she hadn't slept so soundly for months.

Shocked suddenly by the unfamiliar surroundings, she raised herself on one elbow and knew instantly that she was in Ross's bed and covered only by the duvet, and he was nowhere to be seen. The carry-cot which had held Jason in the back room now stood empty beside the bed.

Beth threw back the covers and rushed to the bathroom, then, dressed in the uniform she'd worn the day before, ran downstairs.

'Morning, sleepyhead,' Ross greeted her warmly from the kitchen, a contented Jason resting against his shoulder.

'I'd no idea it was so late.' Beth was panicking. 'Shouldn't you be at the surgery?'

'Dave is covering for me. Sit down and have some breakfast.' He lifted a pot of coffee off its hotplate with his free hand. 'Cereal? Or toast?'

'Just coffee, please.' Beth was desperately trying to recall the events of the previous night. She'd been upset, and Ross had carried her through to his bed to talk. But she didn't remember much discussion. She felt herself colouring hotly at the thought of the events she did recall, and wondered what had taken place after Ross had left her in his bed to answer Jason's cry of distress.

She raised her eyes reluctantly to discover him watching her with amusement. He was aware that she didn't remember, that she knew she had woken to find herself naked in his bed, but, try as she might, remembered nothing else.

Attempting to hide her confusion, she asked, 'So what are the plans for today?'

'I'll leave Jason with you and pop down to the hospital to collect his next feed. When we know what's happening there we can work something out. And get something solid inside you while I'm gone. You need more than coffee to start the day.'

She settled down on to a kitchen chair, chatting to Jason as she cuddled him. Gradually the baby's eyelids drooped and she placed him in his carry-seat.

'What now?' she asked herself, opening a pack of cornflakes and nibbling a few. 'Just what is Ross McKava expecting of me?'

She poured herself another coffee, then tidied the kitchen, all the time wondering how to handle the day ahead.

She was no nearer a solution when she heard his car return, though she was sure it was as well that he hadn't been away long. Otherwise, at the rate her thoughts were whirling, her sanity might have been in question.

He breezed into the kitchen. 'Great news, love. Andrew is showing signs of improvement. Very slight, but they're there. Mr Cavington is going home soon and, when he's taken his wife a change of clothes, will take charge of Jason. 'Good, isn't it? We'll have the rest of the day to ourselves.'

Beth was delighted about Andrew but otherwise she thought it was anything but good news. If Jason didn't need them, the sooner they returned to a normal pattern of behaviour the better.

'We'll leave Jason with his dad, then have a leisurely lunch at the Swan.'

Beth started to protest, but he held up a hand to stop her. 'You can't get out of it. You promised, remember?'

It was about the only thing she did remember. It was now or never. She needed to broach the subject that was uppermost in her mind.

'Ross?'

'Mmm?' She was sure that he knew what she wanted to say but wasn't going to help.

'About last night?'

'Ye-es,' he drawled. 'What about it?'

'Did—er—did Jason take a long time to settle?'

'Not really.'

'Oh!'

'Why do you ask?' he enquired innocently, although Beth was sure that she could detect a gleam of amusement in his eyes.

'I must have fallen asleep before you came back.' There. She'd said it. Now he had to admit what had happened one way or the other.

'I don't usually have that effect on women.' He was laughing at her now. 'If you're trying to find out what happened I can tell you. Absolutely nothing. You were dead to the world and remained so. I thought about disturbing you, but I recalled Tracey telling me that you believed lovemaking should only take place within a stable relationship.'

Damn the man's infallible memory. She *had* said that. Why could he never forget anything?

'And I have to say that I agree. I guess we wouldn't have been able to work together had we gone on.'

Embarrassed, Beth lowered her eyes, but Ross wasn't going to let her get away with that. He raised her head and, searching her face, asked, 'Disappointed? Because I certainly was.'

Beth shook her head emphatically and he released her gaze abruptly. 'I don't believe you, but I guess it's not important.' He started to collect together Jason's bits and pieces without looking at her again.

Her heart sank at his words. His disappointment was at the lost opportunity. He'd just admitted as much, and that she personally wasn't important to him. Thank goodness she'd told him she wasn't disappointed.

'Anything I can do to help?' Beth half-heartedly

picked up some of the baby's paraphernalia, then dropped it again as she remembered the nappy she'd placed in the washing machine. 'I guess I could do some washing.'

'It's all done,' came Ross's terse reply.

Beth looked at him. 'When?'

'I've been up since Jason woke at five. I told you child-rearing is a full-time job.'

'Don't start that again,' Beth said irritably. 'I didn't intend to sleep in. You're trying to make me feel guilty.'

He seemed exasperated. 'Guilt doesn't come into it. That's the prerogative of the career woman—which you tell me you're not.'

He obviously didn't expect an answer and she uttered the thought that was at that moment uppermost in her mind. 'But I am guilty. My staying here last night was a mistake.'

He raised an eyebrow at her unexpected statement. 'Probably.'

Damn the man; he wasn't helping her a bit. 'Joining you for lunch at the Swan would be an even greater one.'

'Probably, but you can't break your promise now.'

'I'm sorry, Ross, but I'm doing just that.'

'Because you're allowing your past to stop you living in the present, or just because you like to get your own way about everything?'

'Because I think it would be a mistake. That's all.'

'And what about me?' he asked bitterly. 'Am I to be discarded as so much chaff?'

Beth really looked at him for the first time that morning, and the hurt she read in his eyes made her flinch. Sure that he'd seen the previous night as nothing more than an opportunity for casual sex, she hadn't considered for one moment that his feelings might match her own.

'Oh, Ross, I'm sorry. I didn't think——'

'No,' he interrupted bitterly. 'You never do. You career women expect the best of both worlds.'

'I told you on my first day,' she retorted hotly, 'that I don't belong in any category. I'm an individual. Not a feminist or a career woman—just someone who takes a pride in her work.'

'And doesn't consider the repercussions of her actions.'

Beth glared at him, aghast at what he was saying. 'How dare you?' Close to tears at his accusations, she scurried upstairs and stuffed her belongings into her bag. She could take a hint as well as the next person. She should never have allowed herself to be manoeuvred into this impossible situation. Working with Ross would be a nightmare from now on.

The telephone rang and she heard Ross answer it, then race up the stairs. 'Beth, where are you?'

Brushing away her angry tears, she came out on to the landing. 'What's the matter? Is it Andrew?'

'No. It was Dave. Kylie's missing—her mother

rang the surgery in a dreadful state.' He must have seen the evidence of her tears but he made no comment. 'Apparently she's gone off with Mrs Wold, but her mother doesn't know where.'

Beth gasped involuntarily. 'Oh, no — that's my fault.'

'Don't talk rubbish,' Ross responded dismissively. 'You've worked wonders with the girl.'

She snorted derisively. 'You wouldn't say that if you knew what set off last week's attack.'

He frowned. 'What's that to do with anything?'

'She wouldn't have had the attack if it hadn't been for me. Mrs Wold wanted to visit and Mum refused. Kylie was upset by the ensuing row.'

'I still don't understand how that makes you responsible.'

'Mrs Wold? Remember? She came to visit me that first Monday morning and when she complained that she never saw Kylie I suggested it was easier for her to go to them than vice versa.'

'So?' Ross appeared untroubled. 'You were right.'

'Not if it caused more tension.'

Ross was thoughtful. 'Did Kylie want to see her?'

Beth nodded.

'That's the cause of the trouble, then, not your suggestion.'

'You're only trying to make me feel better.'

Suddenly overcome by emotion at the rapid sequence of events that was disrupting her life,

Beth again felt tears welling up in her eyes.

'I'm sorry, Ross. I seem to spell trouble for everyone I come into contact with. As soon as you can find a replacement I'll go back to work for the agency.'

Pulling her close, he groaned, before gently wiping the moisture from her cheek and dropping a light kiss on to her lips. 'Of course you don't. I shouldn't have put you in this position. What I said earlier was said in the heat of the moment.'

Maybe, but you said it, Beth thought.

'You've just been through a bad patch.' His voice was filled with gentle understanding, which made her want to cry again. 'Now, I suggest you go and see Mrs Rennell and try and calm her down. I'll take Jason back to his father then I'll join you and we can decide what can be done about Kylie.'

By the time she had washed her tear-stained face Ross had packed the car and was carrying Jason's carry-seat out to strap it in. She checked to see that nothing was left. 'Shall I close the door?'

He nodded. 'I'm ready if you are.'

'As ready as I'll ever be,' she muttered to herself, closing the door firmly on a humiliating episode she wanted to forget.

He watched her closely as she climbed into the passenger seat, and, obviously sensing the turmoil within her, asked, 'Would you rather come with me and then we can see Mrs Rennell together?'

'No. I'm the one who should sort it out. If you

drop me at the surgery I can drive straight over there.'

As she climbed from his car Ross called, 'Wait a moment. I'll jot down my mobile phone number in case you need it. I'll come over to the house as soon as I've handed Jason over, but if the situation should change in the meantime let me know immediately.'

CHAPTER TEN

HER mind only half on what Ross was saying, Beth nodded and, taking the piece of paper, unlocked her own car and climbed in.

Mrs Rennell was dancing agitatedly on the doorstep when she arrived. Beth took her arm gently and led her inside, seating her on a kitchen chair. 'I'll make us a cup of tea,' she told the distressed mother as she filled the kettle.

Between sobs Mrs Rennell told her what had happened.

'Kylie had another attack this morning and now she's gone off without any of her machines. I keep ringing and ringing Jean's number—that's Ken's aunt—but there's no answer. She's been pestering to visit, so, as I was desperate to pop out this morning, I rang her first thing.'

Mrs Rennell gulped back an extra-large sob before continuing, 'She seemed pleased when I asked her to stay with Kylie. I left them for less than an hour. I wasn't keen on her coming in the first place, but Kylie wanted to see her so much,' she sobbed. 'I never thought she'd do anything like this—I thought she was trying to help me for once. She's a——'

'We'll sort all this out later,' Beth broke in

hastily. 'Finding Kylie's all that's important at the moment. How bad was her attack and how was she when you left her?'

'Much better. I don't know what brought the attack on. She woke early and I could hear her wheezing so I made her use that spacer thing and she got better almost immediately.'

'Kylie's a sensible girl. I can't think that they've gone very far from all this.' Beth waved her hand over the medical equipment. 'What about her inhalers? Did she take those?'

Mrs Rennell nodded as a fresh outburst of weeping shook her thin body. 'She's taken her bag and they're always in there.'

That was something at least. Beth offered a silent prayer of thanks as she made and poured the tea. 'What about her father? Have you tried ringing him?'

Mrs Rennell shrugged as she sipped the tea Beth had given her. 'I don't know where he's living and as he's a rep I 'spect he's out on the road somewhere.' —

'Doesn't he have a car phone?'

Mrs Rennell shook her head. 'He told me it could only be used for outgoing calls.'

Abandoning that line of questioning, Beth suggested, 'If you let me have Mrs Wold's address I'll pop over there and see what's happening.'

'I'll come with you.'

Beth shook her head. 'It's better if you stay here—in case Kylie returns or rings up.'

Beth soon found the address that Mrs Rennell had written down for her and knocked lightly on the door. When there was no reply she knocked louder, but still no one answered.

Undecided as to what to do next, she hovered on the doorstep.

'You looking for Mrs W?' a wavering voice called.

Beth spun round and saw the head of an elderly lady leaning out from an upstairs window of the adjoining house.

'Yes. Do you know where she is?'

The lady nodded. 'With her lad, I 'spect. She spends a lot of time with him.'

'Do you know where he lives?'

The neighbour looked doubtful. 'I do, but. . . who're you?'

'I'm from Windber surgery. I have a message for Mrs Wold.'

The old lady lifted her glasses and peered down at Beth's uniform, then, seemingly satisfied, said, 'In that case he lives in Tyburn Street. Near the end. A blue door.'

Hoping that she'd find the house from that description, Beth ran back to her Fiesta and drove quickly to Tyburn Street. No one answered her knock on the only blue door she could find, so she walked round to the back door where an angry Mrs Wold confronted her. 'What do you want?'

Beth could see someone who she presumed was

Kylie's father hovering in the background, watching her apprehensively.

'I was hoping to find Kylie here and check she's better.'

'Of course she's all right,' Mrs Wold reassured her loudly, 'now she's where she ought to be.'

A colourful bundle that turned out to be Kylie raced past Mrs Wold and flung herself into Beth's arms. 'She's OK,' she assured her father and great-aunt. 'She won't split on us.' Looking up at Beth, she confided, 'I'm going to stay here with Dad. Forever.'

'Kylie, you've come away without the oxygen and your nebuliser. You haven't even got your spacer. We must get them to you.'

Kylie shook her head vehemently and said, 'I won't have any attacks now I'm with Dad. Mum caused them.'

Worried that the young girl was being turned against her mother, Beth shook her head. 'I don't think that's entirely true; she——'

'I'm not going back.' Kylie was truculent now.

'You don't have to. If you'd just let me telephone——'

'Dad's not on the phone,' Kylie told her triumphantly.

Unsure what to do next, Beth sighed deeply. She could drive off and reveal Kylie's whereabouts, but then she would lose the little girl's trust. Eventually she smiled at Kylie. 'Let's have a chat and see what can be done. Can I come in?'

Mrs Wold seemed reluctant and barred her way.

'Kylie can't stay hidden forever, you know. She has to go to school.'

Mr Rennell moved Mrs Wold gently from the doorway. 'She's right, Jean. Come in, Nurse.'

'She's a sister,' Kylie corrected incongruously.

The moment Ross parked his BMW outside the house it was obvious that Kylie was still missing. Mrs Rennell raced down the path to meet him. 'Have you found her?'

Ross took her arm gently and led her inside. 'Not yet. Hasn't Sister Linkirk been here?'

Mrs Rennell nodded emphatically. 'Yes. She went over to Mrs Wold's house some time ago.'

Knowing that Mrs Wold could be difficult, Ross took out his phone to check if Beth had left any messages at the surgery.

'No. We haven't heard anything from her,' Dave told him.

'If you do can you let me know on the mobile?'

'Will do.'

Ross replaced the telephone in his pocket. 'I'll follow her over to Mrs Wold's and see what's happening.'

'Can I come with you?' Mrs Rennell was becoming more distraught by the minute. 'I can show you where she lives.'

'I really think you'd be better off staying here in case someone tries to contact you. Give me her address while I ask Mary Banks to come over.'

Weeping copiously, Mrs Rennell did as he asked. 'It's awful being here, doing nothing. If Ken's with them I do hope he doesn't hurt your nurse.'

About to ring Mary, Ross swung round and, with a look of disbelief, asked, 'He's not violent, is he?'

'He wasn't, but before he left me he got quite rough. He wanted to take Kylie, you see, and I wouldn't let him.'

Suddenly concerned for Beth's safety, Ross said abruptly, 'I'm leaving now. I'll ring Mary on the way.'

He rushed back to his car and motored away at speed. If Kylie *was* with her father, would he attack Beth if she tried to take the girl away? The thought appalled him and the moment he arrived at the address Mrs Rennell had given him he rushed from the car to pound on the door. There was no answer; nor was there from any of the neighbouring houses.

Increasingly worried for the safety of Beth *and* Kylie, he returned to the car and rang Mary. 'I know it's Saturday, but could you possibly get over to Carina Rennell's house and stay with her? The little girl's missing. I'm doing everything I can to find her, but not getting very far at the moment.'

'I'll go immediately. Have you involved the police?'

'Not yet. You see, we know who she's with. I won't delay you now, though. Mrs Rennell will give you all the details.'

Mary didn't ask any more questions, and Ross rang the surgery again. 'Dave? Can you look up Ken Rennell's address?'

Dave returned moments later. '20 Darwin Road, Windber Gate Estate.'

'That's his old address. It was worth a try, though.'

Trying to hide his despair, he rang Mrs Rennell.

'Have you got news?' she asked breathlessly.

'Not yet, but Mary's on her way over to you. Now, are you sure you have no idea where your ex-husband is living?'

'No, none at all. No one seems to know.'

'Can you remember the details of any of his friends?'

Mrs Rennell supplied him with a couple and, thanking her, he rang off to try and find them.

Neither of them could help him, but the second one he visited gave him the address of another friend, and there Ross struck lucky. The friend told him where Ken was living at the moment, but that he wasn't on the telephone.

Climbing back into the car, Ross muttered to himself, 'Why, oh, why did I let her go on her own?' If anything happened to her it would be his fault. Having guessed that she was emotionally vulnerable, he should have realised that his attempt to liberate her feelings might backfire.

He'd pushed her too far and now there was no knowing how she'd react if Ken Rennell turned violent.

When he got to the address he'd been given he found that house empty as well, and, again, none of the neighbours were at home. His hopes dashed, he rushed back to Darwin Road to see if Mrs Rennell had any news.

He was comparing notes with Mary when he heard a car stop outside. He rushed to the front door. So great was his relief at seeing Beth climbing from her Fiesta unharmed that he raced to meet her, all his fears for her pouring out in a torrent of recrimination.

'Where on earth have you been? Why didn't you wait for me, or at least let me know where you were? I gave you the number of my mobile and——'

'Where have I been?' Beth asked coldly, her eyes wide with disbelief. 'I've been doing my job, sorting out a problem that was partly of my making. You didn't expect me to interrupt what I was doing to find a telephone, did you? Because I can assure you that if I had I wouldn't be here now.'

Beth's furious interruption made him realise that he should be telling her how worried he'd been, but she was so incensed that she refused to listen when he tried.

'You don't believe I'm capable of doing anything off my own bat, do you? At least, not the way you think it should be done. Well, let me tell you, if you'd approached this situation in the way you've just bawled at me you'd have blown it—immediately. It needed a lot of patience to talk Kylie and her father round and persuade them to drop Mrs Wold at her own house before discussing things calmly with Mrs Rennell.'

She shrugged herself free as he tried to catch hold of her arm. 'And here they are. That's Ken Rennell parking his car across the road. You can take over now, and I can assure you it won't be easy. However, you're welcome to take the credit for any success. I'm off to enjoy the rest of my weekend and I wish you the very best of luck. You'll need it.'

She flounced back down the path at speed, and, climbing into the driver's seat of her car, slammed the door with such force that she obviously didn't hear him call, 'Beth, you've got it all wrong. I was desperately worried about you. . .'

Beth drove away knowing that she could never work with Ross McKava again. He would probably sue her for breach of contract, but to subject herself, even temporarily, to his unpredictable moods was unthinkable.

Last night he would willingly have taken advantage of the situation they had found themselves in, and today he could barely be civil to her. Thank goodness Jason had woken when he did.

She let herself into her flat, from which it

seemed that she had been absent much longer than a day, and wrote a letter of resignation, intending to drop it through the surgery door. Then she rang her parents to say that she was on her way home. She'd tell them of her decision to quit when she got there.

She cleaned the flat and defrosted the fridge before carrying her cases out to the car. She would return her keys by post to the letting agent. She stopped only once — to push her resignation through the surgery letter box.

Her parents welcomed her warmly, making little comment about her decision not to return to Windber. Beth guessed that they'd recognised her distress and were allowing her to settle before asking too many questions.

Surprisingly, she slept well for the first time that week and, after doing justice to her mother's Sunday roast lunch, announced that she would take the farm sheepdog out for a walk.

'Do you want me to come?' her father asked tentatively.

She shook her head, knowing that he would ask questions. 'I'll be fine with Penny for company.' Before she could share her problems she needed to think them through herself.

She stopped at a favourite spot, with a distant view across a shallow valley, and, having sampled a couple of strawberries from the adjoining field, settled on the grass beneath a cherry tree with Penny whining at her feet.

She was deep in thought, trying to work out what the future could possibly hold for her now, when Penny pricked up her ears and gave a low growl. Beth swung round, sensing that she wasn't alone, but could see no one. She was about to dismiss the feeling as nonsense when a trace of familiar aftershave wafted past her nose. Certain now that it was her imagination playing tricks, she clambered slowly to her feet, intending to move on.

What she saw as she approached the next field stopped her in her tracks. Ross McKava was looking out across *her* valley—or was he? Was he just a figment of her imagination, conjured up by her troubled mind? She closed her eyes, hoping to make the vision disappear, but when she opened them she discovered that he was solid reality, and walking towards her.

'What are you doing here?' she snapped.

He moved closer, allowing his dark eyes to search her face before replying, 'I came to find you.'

'Why?' she asked tersely.

'To persuade you to withdraw your notice before anyone else has a chance to see it.'

'Why?' Beth was unrelenting in her hostility.

'I think you're making a mistake and I blame myself.'

'Why?' she demanded again.

Ross sighed deeply and gently encircled her with his arms. 'Because I was impatient, and

scared you by using caring for Jason as an excuse
to move in on you too quickly. I recognise that
now and I don't want to lose you, Beth.'

She was immediately defensive. 'Even though
you don't trust my work?'

'You're wrong, Beth,' he told her quietly. 'Now
that I know you I'd trust you with my life.'

She raised her eyes to meet his and, reading
entreaty there, laughed harshly. 'Like yesterday?'

'I wasn't criticising anything you'd done, Beth,
believe me.' He spoke quietly. 'Mrs Rennell had
told me earlier that her husband could be violent
so I was out of my mind with worry. I'd tried to
follow your trail and couldn't get beyond Mrs
Wold's empty house.'

'You should have worn a uniform! Her neighbour obviously didn't think you were someone
who could be trusted with the details of her whereabouts.'

He shook his head ruefully. 'You can't imagine
how I felt not having a clue where you were. That
was why I "bawled" at you, as you put it. I wanted
to come after you and explain, but, if your hard
work wasn't to be in vain, I knew I had to stay.'

Unable to believe him, Beth looked up at him
with narrowed eyes. 'Ken Rennell violent? Come
off it, Ross, he's the gentlest man imaginable.'

'I know that now, but I didn't then, not until
I met him yesterday afternoon and learnt that that
old witch Mrs Wold had caused all the trouble.
She didn't think his wife was good enough for

him so she told Carina that he was having an affair, and persuaded *him* that Carina was unable to cope. Then, would you believe, she told him that Kylie was being ill-treated by her mother?'

'It's incredible what damage one jealous woman can do.' Beth wanted to believe his explanation but it wasn't easy.

'The moment the Rennells made the decision to try again without her influence I sped round to your flat, but I was too late. It was empty. And you weren't there this morning either.

'Then Teri Rolle's mother contacted me to say that Teri was very ill and could I tell her which vaccinations she'd had. I went into the surgery to dig out her notes and discovered your letter.'

Beth asked anxiously, 'What's the matter with her? I did her last injections. Did I do something wrong?'

'Calm down, Beth. It was nothing to do with you. When I eventually got through to the doctors there she was much better and they thought it was probably due to her putting ice in her drinks without checking the source.'

'I warned her about that as well.'

He nodded. 'I know, but it's the old, old story. She told the doctor she'd been warned, but that after a few drinks she forgot.'

Beth sighed with relief and Ross seized the opportunity to move her closer within the circle of his arms.

'So will you withdraw your resignation?'

Although recognising that he genuinely meant what he was saying, Beth was undecided. 'I'm not sure if that would be a good idea. Over the past twenty-four hours I've come to the conclusion that moving to Windber was a big mistake.'

He leant forward and brushed her lips with a kiss. 'Not necessarily, if you can learn to put the past into its proper perspective.'

'If only it were that easy,' she told him bleakly, wishing, not for the first time, that he weren't so darned perceptive.

'If you'll let me I'd like to try and help you do so.'

Unwilling to meet his eyes, she looked down. 'I hardly know you, Ross. And you certainly don't know me.'

'I know enough.'

She shook her head. He wouldn't say that if he knew the mistakes she'd made in the past, she thought. Afraid of him probing deeper, she quickly changed the subject. 'How did you find me?'

'It wasn't difficult. You told me that home was a Larbeth farm. When I found it your mother said that this was your favourite spot.'

'And what else did she tell you?' she asked guardedly.

His reply was gentle. 'As it happens, nothing, although, having seen how worried they are about you, I wonder why you're so reluctant to accept that people care about you.'

'Because I haven't been set a very good example in the past.' She met his gaze with her own, until, detecting a veiled desire there, she started to move away.

He caught hold of her hand to prevent her and surprised and shocked her when he said quietly, 'Your husband was a rep, wasn't he? And he was unfaithful to you. That's why reps are such anathema to you, isn't it?'

'I thought you said my mother hadn't told you anything,' she retorted angrily.

'She didn't, but Carina Rennell said something in passing that made me put two and two together, and I don't think I made five—did I?' His voice was caressingly gentle now.

Beth felt a sudden, overwhelming desire to pour out the grief and resentment she had bottled up for so long, and as she wouldn't be working with Ross in the future it no longer mattered that he knew.

'Richard died in a car crash with his mistress. It was my fault that he started to stray. He didn't want a family.' There, she'd said it—confessed the secret fear that she was the one to blame that had consumed her.

'That's not your fault. It takes two to tango, after all.'

'I know, but accidents happen. And when the baby was stillborn I felt it was retribution for refusing to have an abortion. He wouldn't have left me if I had, and perhaps the accident wouldn't

have happened. I ruined his life.' She stifled a sob.
'I couldn't bear to make the same mistake twice.'

Ross pulled her close to his shoulder and
murmured into her hair, 'What makes you think
you will?'

'How can I be sure I won't?'

'Perhaps this'll go some way to convincing you.'
He leaned forward and kissed her lips gently.
'Mmm, ripe strawberries—delicious. That's
funny because you always remind me of a
bruised fruit.'

'I've been sampling the crops,' she told him to
hide her confusion. Aware that she couldn't prevent a physical response, she wanted to escape,
because, however much he seemed to be offering
at that moment, she didn't feel that she could
survive a similar hurt. 'This is pointless, Ross. We
disagree about everything.'

'Apart from our need for one another.' His
mouth was on hers again, this time hot and
demanding, conveying all his pent-up hunger in
a kiss that took her breath away.

'Oh, Beth, what a fool I've been,' he whispered.
'I think I've loved you from that moment you
accosted me as an intruder.' He searched for her
lips again but Beth turned her head away.

'Ross. . .no, you haven't. You've felt sorry for
me, but that's not the same thing——'

'You're wrong. I wanted to help you, yes, but
only because you appeared to be the girl I've been
searching for, although I wouldn't allow myself

to believe it at first.' He gave a rueful laugh. 'I even tried to find fault with everything you did to prove to myself that you weren't as perfect as you seemed.'

'Ross, I——'

This time he silenced her protest with a finger on her lips. 'You took everything I handed out with an aplomb that shows you *are* exactly what I need. And you can't deny you feel the same. Your body has proved it more than once.'

She was unconvinced. 'I may be physically attracted to you, Ross, but I know only too well that that's not a basis for a successful relationship. That needs agreement on the important issues and we don't have it.'

He grinned. 'Only because we've allowed our pasts to superimpose on the present.'

'I don't think so, Ross. I wasn't a feminist when I came to Windber but your behaviour has pushed me in that direction. Your resentment at my handling Kylie's kidnapping alone, your opinion that it's mandatory for a wife to give up work to rear her family—the list is endless. It could never work.'

He pulled her back into contact with his body before telling her, 'I'm actually proud of the way you handled the Rennell case.' She struggled in vain to escape his hold. 'If it hadn't been for you Mrs Wold's lies would probably have wrecked the lives of all that family.'

Beth was suddenly contrite. 'I should have

asked you about Kylie. How is she coping?'

He reclaimed her lips before murmuring, 'Still concerned for everyone but yourself, eh? She'll survive. She's delighted that her parents are trying to make a go of it.' He searched his pocket. 'I've actually brought you something from Kylie.' He handed her a tightly folded page. 'She was upset when you didn't join us yesterday afternoon, and asked me to give you this. I was waiting for the right moment.'

'And this is it?' she asked suspiciously.

'You read it and see.'

She unfolded the paper and to her embarrassment saw the poem Kylie had shown her in the surgery, now complete. She moved away from him to read it and her cheeks coloured as she reached the last verse:

> If Dr McKava marries his nurse,
> They'll both look after me.
> Until their children need her at home.
> When I hope she'll ask me to tea.

Ross waited quietly until she thoughtfully folded the paper and told him, 'Kylie obviously agrees with you that mothers should stay at home with their children. But I'm telling you now, I don't consider it hurts if the mother has a part-time job as the children grow older; in fact it can be a bonus—she isn't bored out of her mind and so is a more interesting mother when she *is* at home.'

'I can accept that.'

Disbelieving, she looked at him. 'You told me yourself that that was the cause of the split between you and Ruth.'

'Mmm. Perhaps I've learnt something too. I think I always knew Ruth would never interrupt her career, even though I hoped to persuade her otherwise. You're different. Your agonising over losing Naomi tells me that, as well as the expression in your eyes when we talk about babies and children. I guess you say otherwise just to provoke me.'

'You could be very wrong.'

He grinned. 'I don't think so, especially when my patients appear to confirm my views.'

She frowned. 'What do you mean?

'Kylie thinks that, as we always work together, we should marry and have a family. Mrs Cavington kept impressing on me how wonderful you were, and Tracey—remember her?—informed me that you said sex should only take place in a loving relationship. Seems they all thought we needed a push in the right direction!'

'Maybe.' Beth was doubtful.

'You obviously have a family who care about you, and want children of your own. So why let one misjudgement, if that's what it was, affect your whole life?'

She struggled with her memories. She knew that

she was attracted to him, but could she trust him?

He must have sensed her thoughts for he murmured into her hair, 'If you're to have anything of a life you have to learn to trust again. You were unlucky with Richard. I can't believe that, with you feeling as you do, anyone would ask you to have an abortion. We're not all the same, Beth, and I promise I'll never hurt you.'

Wanting to believe him, she looked up with tears in her eyes. 'I—I think I know that, Ross.'

He lowered his lips to hers then, in a kiss that demanded her submission with its searing intensity.

As they sank down on to the grass, her body, crushed beneath his, seemed to have a will of its own. Even as her mind screamed the need to escape her hips arched, as if drawn towards the heat that raged between them, and when he finally released her she knew that the passion they'd shared could only exist within a depth of love she'd never experienced with Richard.

'Now does that convince you we're meant for one another?' He cradled her face between his hands so that she couldn't avoid his gaze.

'Is that a proposal?' she asked suspiciously.

'Not exactly. I need the right place and time for that. So I suggest that we go and tell your mum and dad that you've changed your mind, or rather I've changed it for you. Then we make tracks for Windber as we have an early start in the morning.'

'You mean you'll let me back into the surgery?' she teased. 'You won't seize this opportunity to keep me out of the place for good, as you managed to do on my first day?'

Ross took her letter of resignation from his pocket and tore it into small pieces. 'Because of a problem with the previous nurse I wanted to train you my way from the beginning. As I was out of the surgery that day I didn't trust Liz and Dave not to swamp you with unsuitable work.'

'Liz told me about the ectopic pregnancy.' When he raised his eyebrows in surprise she added, 'I wish you'd explained in the beginning, though, when you were putting me through the third degree during our meal at the pub!'

'Third degree?' He grinned at her sheepishly. 'I wasn't that bad, was I?'

When she didn't answer he lifted her chin gently so that he could read her expression. 'I see that I was. So I'll make amends immediately. We can be back at the Swan for that haddock *au gratin* you promised to share.'

When she hesitated he added cryptically, 'It might even turn out to be the right time and place.'

Beth retorted hotly, 'With Mike around? After you practically accused me of flirting with him?'

'I surprised myself when I did that! I knew nothing about you apart from the fact that you wore a wedding-ring, and I suppose subconsciously I didn't want to believe you were the type to behave that way when you were already married.'

'As if I would,' Beth retorted indignantly.

'You won't get the chance.' He swept her up into his arms and claimed her lips with a kiss that sent her heart racing. 'Because, on second thoughts, I've decided we'll forgo the haddock and have another take-away instead, followed by a quiet night in, but this time undisturbed by babies or nightmares from the past. What do you say?'

Suddenly almost sure that she wasn't about to make another mistake, Beth murmured softly, 'I think there's nothing I'd like better, apart from a regular repeat performance.'